Christmas Tree Wars

A Novel

DELORES TOPLIFF

Published by Scrivenings Press LLC
15 Lucky Lane
Morrilton, Arkansas 72110
https://ScriveningsPress.com

Printed in the United States of America

Paperback ISBN 978-1-64917-151-1

eBook ISBN 978-1-64917-152-8

Library of Congress Control Number: 2021945206

Editor: K. Banks

Cover by Linda Fulkerson, www.bookmarketinggraphics.com.

All scriptures are taken from the KING JAMES VERSION (KJV): KING JAMES VERSION, public domain.

All characters are fictional, and any resemblance to real people, either factual or historical, is purely coincidental.

ACKNOWLEDGMENTS

I'm thankful my Savior found me early, leads me safely, and put a love for story in my heart.

Thanks to Patricia Bradley and Beth K. Vogt—author friends who stand with me daily in the trenches.

To Susan May Warren and her How to Write A Novel organization and its prayer huddles.

To my KCW Mentoring group friends who beautifully critique and pray for each other. Y'all also teach me fun Southern sayings and ways.

To Wisconsin family and friends who taught me to love the area and history—Aaron, Jen, and girls; Patti and Tim; Mary and Greg; Cave of the Mounds; Summers Christmas Tree Farm.

To Jean Ann Carlson Sharpe and family for years of fun learning to "raise the Swedish flag" and to enjoy Svenska ways of doing things.

To lovely Norwegian and Danish friends like Jane, Allan, and children. You make me happy to include Scandinavian blood as part of my heritage.

Thanks to my sister, Nancy Williams, for excellent, dedicated proofreading.

Many thanks to Kaci Banks for editing with fine touches and suggestions that made this a better book.

I loved working college summers for the U.S. Forest Service in Washington State and later for B.C. and Alberta Canada Forest Services doing forest fire support including driving through fire lines plus flying over incredible scenery in spotter planes. I actually considered a Forest Service career.

For those who love the warmth of Hallmark Christmas movies, *Christmas Tree Wars,* by Delores Topliff, will be a holiday favorite. Topliff has crafted a heartfelt tale full of joy, faith, and family, centered around a hometown rivalry that will delight her readers.

— Gabrielle Meyer, author of When the Day Comes

Offering a fascinating inside look at Christmas tree farms, Topliff's *Christmas Tree Wars* is a sweet story of two feuding families who come together to claim the best prize of all—love. With charming characters and a setting where the scent of spruce nearly lifts off the pages, *Christmas Tree Wars* is a story you'll want to add to your holiday collection.

— Lisa Jordan, award-winning author for Love Inspired

1

Kris Lundquist jingled the change in his pocket and looked through his 15th story window over Rockefeller Plaza. He weighed a decision and glanced at his calendar. So far, 1966 had been a good year for him. Would he stay in New York City these next two weeks building more accounts? Or fly home to his parents' Christmas tree farm to help them through a financial crisis? He'd come a long way from Balsam, Wisconsin, population 1924.

His eyes returned to the window. Although his office space and window were small, he never tired of his million-dollar view. He checked the meeting planner on his desk and reviewed his schedule for the next two weeks.

August was almost gone. Should he focus on the Greenshaw account? No, it was on track. Mandeville and Sykes? They were on track and moving forward as well. The Hutchinson Trust? He smiled. They loved his new health benefits package and promised final approval soon. He'd delivered impressive account growth last quarter and had a nice bonus check to prove it. His employer, Morgan Guthrie of Guthrie and Associates, was pleased and vocal about bigger and better plans. Maybe including a new office with a bigger view.

Kris picked up the photo of Mom and Dad on the other corner of his desk. Standing in front of their Lundquist Christmas Tree Farms sign, arms around each other and smiling for the camera, they were his two favorite people on Earth. But ... Kris couldn't understand how Dad had landed in financial trouble again since the farm had so much going for it. Still, if returning home for two weeks could make the difference, Kris would do that for them. He made up his mind and made the call.

"Mr. Guthrie? You know the possible trip we talked about? I do need two weeks off. I'm ahead on projects and will do some work by phone. Yes, flying tomorrow to include the Labor Day weekend. I'll make up more time when I'm back."

Minutes later, he smiled and disconnected. Tomorrow he'd be in Balsam with two weeks to turn his parents' Christmas tree farm around.

Next, Kris dialed home, his smile warming his voice. "Dad? I've worked it out. But don't tell Mom."

"Coming tomorrow but don't want me to tell her? She'll kill me, and I like living."

Kris held his phone away from his ear as his father almost shouted. Was he getting hard of hearing?

"If you tell her, she'll start a housecleaning frenzy and claim there's nothing to eat, which is never true."

Dad gusted a sigh. "I'll try. She's out collecting chicken eggs now, but she's practically clairvoyant. She's probably heard every word. Which airport?"

"I tried Duluth, but they're out of car rentals because of Labor Day."

"You don't need a car. Fly into the Twin Cities and drive our farm truck while you're here."

"No, I don't want you to make a trip all the way into Minneapolis."

"I'm heading to Hudson for hardware anyway, and it's a straight shot from there." For several seconds there was silence. "I'm glad you're coming, but why now?"

"Because you helped me through school. It's about time I do something to repay you for all the support you gave. I help other people through financial troubles. Why not you?"

Dad blew a raspberry. "How much time you got? Three months? Four?"

"No. Barely two weeks. If we can't turn things around by then, maybe you should sell out and take an eight to five job."

"I'm not ready for that."

Kris sucked in a breath. "You know I love our farm, but it has to pay for itself, or taxes will eat it up."

"Some years it pays, but it's hard. If you can turn things around in two weeks, I'll agree you're the genius people say you are."

Kris chuckled. "We'll see. I'll phone you my flight details later. See you soon."

The next day, memories of home overflowed Kris's heart as his Boeing 727 broke through clouds to descend over evergreen-forested hills into the Minneapolis-St. Paul airport. The nearly four-hour flight from Idlewild wasn't a long enough transition from big city financial wars to small-town Christmas tree farm challenges. Each trip, Kris promised to return sooner, but big-city demands interfered.

After landing and deplaning, Kris grabbed his carry-on and rushed through the baggage doors. Yup, Dad stood leaning against the Lundquist Christmas Tree Farms pick-up truck. They flung their arms around each other in backslapping hugs.

"You're a sight for sore eyes, big fella. Welcome home." Dad wiped his eyes.

"Great to be here." Kris threw his carry-on into the back and climbed into the front. He took a closer look at Dad.

"Are you doing okay?"

"Sure, just tired."

Dad looked older since Easter, with deeper lines tunneling his face. How old would he be next birthday? Was something going on with him physically besides the finances?

"Mom didn't want to ride to Hudson?" Kris asked.

"Nope." Dad started his engine. "She says hardware shopping isn't her thing."

He eased into traffic and turned onto Hwy. 494 East. "You brought work clothes and boots?"

"Sure. I'm ready for Christmas tree fresh air."

"Better than Big Apple fumes?"

"You know it. A thousand times." Kris rolled down his window and inhaled. Why did Dad look guilty? "What aren't you telling me?"

"Okay, I fess up. I had to tell Mom. She would have scalped me, and I don't have hair to lose." He doffed his farm cap. "She's cooking up a storm for her number one son."

"Her *only* son, Dad. You both overdo it."

"When you're a dad, you will, too."

"That won't be any time soon. First I'd have to find someone to build a life with, and they keep me pretty busy at work."

After listening to Dad talk non-stop for forty miles, Kris stared through the truck window at the final highway curve before the first glimpse of Balsam.

"There's still no place like home."

Dad heaved a sigh. "Son, I would have been okay if Norway spruce prices had held up and we didn't have that cursed blight."

"That's the thing about farming. No guarantees."

Past the sign reading, *Welcome to Balsam, Wisconsin's Christmas Tree Capital,* Dad's truck brakes hissed as he pulled to the curb in front of the town's grocery store.

"Mom needs whipping cream for your pie. Wanna come?"

"Might as well."

Dad was still tall, lanky, and strong, but couldn't shed the spare tire around his middle. In fact, he might have gained since Easter, which likely strained his heart.

Kris studied him. "Are you on an exercise program?"

"I don't need an *exercise program.* I work hard, Mr. City Boy."

"That's not getting rid of your stomach."

Dad patted his paunch.

"I should cut back, but it's hard with Mom's good cooking. She thinks if she cooks her best, you'll come home more."

"Ridiculous." Kris snapped his fingers. "That has nothing to do with it."

"We know that, but it's how she thinks."

Rain started, and Dad climbed out and pulled a tarp over the hardware items in his pick-up bed. Kris jumped out of the truck to help.

"So, your job's going good?"

Kris shrugged. "Not bad. Guthrie's pleased. I'll do a little phone work from here."

"Not much, I hope. I'll keep you plenty busy."

Dad had just opened the grocery store door when a whirling human mass struck his middle like a bowling ball.

"I've had it with you, Lundquist." The small man grabbed Dad's arm. "You have some explaining to do about what you said at the last Chamber of Commerce meeting."

Kris narrowly avoided falling onto the men as Dad jerked free.

"Stow it, Halvorsen. My son just got home."

The smaller man stopped and stared. "Kris?"

Kris nodded. The guy was bundled up, but he recognized their neighbor, owner of the original farm they'd bought their land from at auction.

"I don't care who's home. This town's too small for both of us." His spindly neck swiveled like a turkey gobbler. "For a newcomer, you act like you own the place!"

Newcomer? Kris stiffened. "We've owned our place fourteen years!"

"Another time, Halvorsen." Dad reopened the door that had closed.

Halvorsen's face deepened to purple. If he were a match, he would have exploded. Several shoppers stopped to watch.

"Uncle Hal!"

Kris's gaze swept past the older man to a young woman approaching with a frown on her heart-shaped face. Memory stirred. Those soft auburn curls. Wait, was this Marcie? Halvorsen's gangly niece he'd played tricks on in her teens until that summer when they'd been an item? She wasn't gangly now. His mind updated old images with the lovely woman standing before him. He should never have lost track of her—she was a knock-out.

"Marcie, you look great."

She tilted her head. "You, too, Kris."

Her uncle poked Kris's dad's chest. "Skip the niceties, Lundquist. Just because you folks came along when I had to sell half our place doesn't make us neighbors. After I win this year's state tree growing contest, I'll have money. Then, if you're any kind of Christian, you'll sell your half back at the same price."

He hunched his neck like a turtle withdrawing into its shell.

Kris's dad squared his shoulders. "Halvorsen, you can't seriously expect me to do that. Your place was for sale, and I bought it fair and square."

"Except you shouldn't have." Halvorsen's arms flared like he would strike while Dad's stiffened his against his sides. "If I offer enough money, you'll sell. Besides, Marcie's home from university now to cure our blight. We'll turn things around so fast, we'll leave you in the dust." He thrust out his chin.

"Uncle Hal!" Face ablaze, Marcie took his arm.

Dad turned from Halvorsen to her "Wait. You're Marcie? The little girl in pigtails?"

"That's right."

Ouch. Dad should have at least said, "the cute little girl in pigtails," because she was.

"It's been a long time." Her expression held none of her uncle's rancor.

Dad blinked. "Either you've been away too long, or we haven't crossed paths when you're home."

"Both." Her shoulders eased. "I've been tied up because my

forestry course runs year-round. I'm only home to help now because I can do my last semester from home."

"Like Kris is here two weeks to help us." When Dad offered his hand, Marcie took it.

Kris did the same and let his grip linger a moment.

"You know where we live, Marcie. Come see us."

"I doubt that's wise." She reclaimed her hand.

"Forget that," her uncle growled. "They're on the other half of our land. Tears me up every time I see them."

"It's been fourteen years, Uncle Hal. Time to forget and move on."

"Never!" He blew through his lips like a horse resisting a saddle. "Not until we get our land back."

"You sold it, and my dad bought it." Kris spread his hands open to show it was simple math and then turned to Marcie. "You're studying Forestry?"

"Nursery management. I graduate next June. You?"

"I graduated in business and then an MBA from University of Minnesota. Now I'm a financial planner in New York City."

"And climbing the ladder fast," Dad said with pride.

Her eyebrows lifted. "Impressive."

Kris shook his head. "Not so much. Mostly hard work."

Marcie's uncle waved a fist. "You went to Minnesota? Figures. Too good for a Wisconsin school, like Marcie. And I suppose you're a Vikings fan!"

Kris froze at the acid in Halvorsen's tone.

"Does it matter?"

"Sure as shootin' it matters."

"Uncle Hal!" Marcie tugged his arm. "Our schools are partners. They help each other."

"Not the way I see it. They're rivals, just like Lundquist and me. Always will be, and I keep track."

"Maybe you shouldn't." Her tone stayed gentle, but she tugged his arm harder. A few nervous customers eased around them. "Let's go, Uncle Hal. We're blocking the entrance."

During Halvorsen's outbursts, Kris watched Marcie. Her shoulder-length auburn hair swung as she spoke, its red highlights accenting her emerald eyes. Her cheeks flushed, either from the day's cool temperature or her uncle's behavior.

Her green slacks and jacket complemented her coloring. Kris glanced down at his clothing and wanted to sigh. He'd worn a coat and tie on the plane but removed both as soon as he got in Dad's truck. In rolled-up shirtsleeves now, he wished he'd worn the dress shirt Mom had mailed for his birthday instead. Plus, on the flight, he'd managed to spill food on one pant leg, making him wish he were anywhere else on the planet right now. He slid that leg behind the other. Mom had often said, "Always dress your best. You never know who you might meet." This was vacation. He was not at work. Still, he wished he had listened.

After checking her watch, Marcie hooked her arm through her uncle's, managing him as easily as a skilled trainer turns a high-strung horse. "We need to get Aunt Ingrid. We can't keep her waiting."

Marcie's words snapped her uncle awake. His lips firmed. "We'll talk again, Lundquist. May the best man win."

Dad nodded. "I hope we both do well."

Kris exhaled a long breath as he watched Halvorsen and his niece cross the parking lot. Her uncle took the passenger side of a dented pick-up while Marcie slid into the driver's seat.

"All of that to stop for whipping cream," Dad said. "I'd better get it now so we can get out of here."

As they paid, Dad pulled truck keys from his pocket and dangled them. "Want to drive, son?"

"Sure. I'd like that." They climbed into the truck. "Wow, Marcie has grown up!" Kris said.

His dad chuckled. "Most folks do. I admit, she turned out well. I'm sure Ingrid is happy to have someone cheerful around."

"I'll bet. What's going on with them, anyway? Halvorsen seems tense enough for a mental health check."

"I know. Today is the worst I've seen him. His finances are

down, plus his wife is feeling puny. Some kind of sickness the doctors haven't diagnosed."

Kris flashed the turning signal and eased onto the street. "Sorry to hear. Who would have thought there'd be more drama in Balsam than New York theaters lit with neon lights? Are things really that bad?"

"Depends on who you ask. Worse for some." Dad lifted his green Lundquist Christmas Farms cap and combed his thinning hair with his fingers before slapping his cap back on. "Everyone's hurting. I don't fully know Halvorsen's situation, but the blight hit him hard with him only growing Norway spruce. We're more diversified, which puts us in better shape. Plus, the other half of this year's property taxes come due this month, which pressures us all before we get sales. But I should hush. Mom told me not to burden you with our stuff."

"Burden me?" Kris laid a hand on his dad's arm. "We're family. Besides, how can I help solve your problem if you don't tell me what's going on?"

"But your life's in New York now." Dad hiked an eyebrow. "It sounds like you're getting chummy with the boss's daughter."

"Laura? Maybe." Kris's gaze surveyed Main Street's historic buildings and then returned to the road. "It's too soon to tell. I love Balsam, just wish there were more opportunities here. Once you phoned, I had to come."

"Thanks. I'm glad your boss let you off."

"I had to push a little, but he values people helping family. He should appreciate loyalty in someone getting serious with his daughter, don't you think?"

Dad nodded. "Definitely."

Kris lightly punched his dad's arm. "Hey, I learned from the best."

They shared a laugh.

"Say, I almost forgot," Dad said. "We need to stop at the post office for two rolls of stamps for our Christmas mailing."

"That many customers?"

"I'm building our list."

"Sounds good." Kris entered the parking area and braked at the sight of a familiar dented truck. "Oh, no. The Halvorsens are here."

Dad craned his neck. "They're allowed. It's a free country, but I don't want to see Halvor again today. It looks like Marcie's getting out. If you park on the far side and he stays in the truck, we might be okay."

"I hope so. Our encounter earlier was more than enough."

"He's not usually that bad. We've had decent conversations, just not lately. Something more must be going on."

2

Marcie eased away from the curb to drive to the post office and waited for her uncle to calm.

"What happened when you saw him in the store? I've never seen you so riled."

He swiped a hand over his stubbled face. "Did I go too far?"

"I think you know you did."

"Yeah, I guess. But I just can't help it." He slapped the dashboard. "It's Lundquist. He brings out the worst in me. Now he owns half the land our relatives cleared and homesteaded for years." He flexed his hands and grimaced. "I've worked my fingers to the bone all these years, and for what? We're further behind all the time instead of ahead. My money disappears while everything he touches turns to gold. I should call him King Midas."

"But he's having trouble, too. That's why Kris came home."

"Lundquist doesn't have trouble compared to me, but I was surprised to see Kris."

"I wish you hadn't torn into Lars like a bowling ball knocking down pins."

"Ya." He rubbed his head. "I bulldozed his shoulder so hard I hurt my head."

"I'll bet." Marcie suppressed a laugh.

"I know I only have myself to blame."

"Why are you more upset now than usual?"

He squinted. "You really want to know?"

"Would I ask if I didn't?"

"Here's why." He spread empty hands. "Our business is doing worse than you know. I'm behind on payments and haven't even posted all our debts in the ledger yet. I'm sorry it's this way, but everything depends on this season. The bank's threatening to call in my loan. If I don't make a big payment by Christmas, they'll evict us after the first of the year. I haven't told your aunt yet."

Marcie swallowed. "That's awful. Please don't while she's not feeling well. But be honest with me so I can help."

"Ya. I need to be honest with somebody." His head dropped to his chest. "Even if you find a miracle cure for spruce blight today, it's too late. If I don't send a large payment by the end of December, they'll start foreclosure."

"There's no leeway or alternate plan?"

"They say not." He tossed his head. "And I thought those bankers were my friends. We served on Chamber of Commerce committees together. I bought girl scout cookies from their kids." His voice broke.

"They have a job to do." Marcie tried to comfort. "I'm sure it's hard for them, too."

He pulled his red farm hankie from his pocket and twisted it. "I can't lose the land we have left. It's sacred. Great Grandpa Halvorsen homesteaded it himself straight off the boat."

"You think we could lose all of it?"

"I'm afraid so. His first home was a shanty. He cut timber and grubbed roots out of the ground." As her uncle lifted his head to stare through the windshield, both his hands shook. "It broke my heart to sell the first half. I couldn't survive losing the rest."

"They might seriously sell off the whole thing? Uncle, you

must let me know things like that." Her quick intake of breath made the steering wheel lurch and the tires crossed the painted line. She almost clipped the corner edge of the bank's clock tower.

"No use trying to break into the bank that way," Halvor quipped, then grew serious again. "I hoped to find an answer without you and Ingrid knowing."

"There must be some way to save things, something we haven't thought of yet."

He shook his head no. "I've searched and tried everything I know. I don't have any ideas left."

"We'll think and pray. Like you told the Lundquists—with me home, we'll work hard enough, long enough, to turn things around." *Lord, make that true.*

"Thanks, Marcie. I'd like to believe that. Thanks for being willing. I don't want you worried."

"But that's part of belonging to a family."

His head jerked. "I guess. By the way, Ingrid added you to our payroll. It isn't much each month, but we'll share what comes in."

"Don't do it now, not while we're in trouble." She patted his arm. "My university work-study grants cover me this term." *Well, that's mostly true.* "Maybe pay me later when things improve."

"It's already set up. We won't change our minds."

Her chin jutted. "You're a stubborn Norwegian."

"You're another."

She smiled back at him for a moment before returning her eyes to the road.

"I'll never forget what you did for Mom and me after Dad died. Even more after Mom got sick." Marcie shook her head. "We couldn't have survived on our own. I'm glad to help now."

He swiped his eyes.

"I hope you both know what you mean to me. You and Aunt Ingrid spoiled me with college care packages with extra to share. I was the envy of my dorm."

"We had fun." He grinned. "That was mostly your aunt."

"But you paid for it, and my best-cook-in-the-world aunt made fabulous goodies," Marcie added. "I want to learn from her and help her now."

"Follow her around more, and her skills will rub off. I've kept you too busy helping me outside."

"It's been fine. We'll make both work."

As they drove along Main Street, Marcie braked at the town's only traffic light.

"It's that durned spruce blight," Uncle Halvor said, chafing his rough hands. "It's ruining me. We'll leave you the farm when that time comes. I just hope there's something left." He blinked a few times, and his voice caught.

"Don't talk like that, Uncle. God will help us."

"I hope so, but it's hard. It seems like He's showing up late." He coughed into his sleeve, and his chest rattled.

"Sometimes it's the last minute. I'll just believe enough for both of us," Marcie said.

"Thanks. We'll know soon enough. Did I mention stopping at the post office before the clinic? I can't forget."

"No, but I will. What do we need?"

"Three rolls of stamps for early Christmas mailers."

She entered the post office parking lot. "Let me run in. You stay here and rest. I'll just be a minute."

The crease between his eyebrows lessened. "Now that you mention it, that sounds good." He reached for his wallet. "Here's money for three rolls."

She waved a hand. "I've got it. We'll settle up later. Three rolls? You're mailing three hundred?"

"Yeah. I'm contacting all possibilities to chase the sales we need."

"Okay, if you think that big a project is justified."

"I have to try."

She nodded. "I'll hurry. Then once we get Aunt Ingrid, we'll drive straight home. I don't think she'll feel like doing anything more after today's tests.

"For sure she won't. She didn't want me there. Told me to run errands." He quit talking and swallowed hard.

"She doesn't want you to worry."

"But she's my wife! We need answers." As he closed his eyes and leaned back, the taut lines in his face softened. "Thanks, Marcie. I am beat."

She closed the truck door with a thunk, nearly colliding with Kris as he hurried toward the building from the far side of the lot.

"Sorry, I almost knocked you down," he said.

She spun to see if Uncle Halvor saw. Thankfully, his eyes were closed.

She climbed the steps, and Kris opened the door for her. "We have to stop meeting at front doors like this." He quirked a smile.

"I know. Twice in one day after years apart."

He paused. "Sorry about that scene at the grocery store. I'm not sure what set your uncle off, but he clearly has it rough these days. I'm sure having you home will help."

"I hope so. It's not like him to get that upset."

They had barely entered the post office when Kris's dad followed them inside.

"Son, I forgot to give you these letters to mail. Got to pay our bills on time as long as we can."

"Sure, Dad."

Marcie looked from one to the other. The grown-up Kris looked more like his handsome father, except for Kris lacking the fine lines edging Lars's blue eyes from years in sun and wind. She liked the cheery Christmas tree logo stitched on Lars's Lundquist Christmas Farms hat. She must design one for their farm. Kris's thick, wavy blond hair in a stylish cut looked great without a hat.

"Last winter's blight hit us all," Lars said, "but your uncle got the worst of it since Norway spruce is what he mostly grows."

"True." Marcie frowned. "I sent him a hundred experimental seedling trees of a blight-resistant trial variety from our university nursery, but he says he'll stick with what he knows and what's worked in the past. He resists new ideas, and trees grow so slowly, it's hard to convince him anything new could be better. He's counting on us finding an answer to the problem."

"I hope you do. And most older guys get stuck in their ways." Kris rolled his eyes.

Lars stepped forward. "Hey, be kind. Some of us old-timers try new ways. Marcie, that's what got your uncle so upset at the last Chamber of Commerce meeting. I mentioned diversifying Christmas tree varieties, and you would have thought I suggested treason. He accused me of destroying tradition. Things got even worse when they elected me president to take over from him in January."

"I'm sure." Marcie winced. "He or his dad have been president here almost since the chamber started."

"I offered to work out a smooth transition with him, but he says he can't work with me."

"That's a shame. Please give him time. I hope he'll come around. He's afraid of change and doesn't handle it well." She smiled so much her eyes crinkled. "I can't believe he still calls you a newcomer after fourteen years here. I think the biggest thing he's got against you is that you're not Norwegian."

"You're right about that." Lars spread his hands in surrender. "But there's not much I can do about it. Norway and Sweden fought wars in the old country, but we don't need to do that here."

The post office line slowly advanced to the only wicket being manned.

"They only have one person on duty?" Kris asked.

"It looks that way. After all, this is Balsam," she said. "Small-town benefits without big city efficiency."

"True, but that can be impersonal and over-rated. Balsam is home. I was seven when we came. Nothing before that compared to living here."

"I know. I was nine when Mom and I came," Marcie said. "You'd already been here several years, but it's home for me, too." She surveyed all six handsome feet of Kris. He'd grown up fine.

"I kind of remember when you came." His voice warmed. "You belong here. Sorry for the hard stuff you've gone through."

"Thanks. It was tough, but it's okay." She would *not* let her eyes fill. She took a breath instead. "It's been long enough that the loss hurts less now. Besides, I couldn't have a better family than Halvor and Ingrid have been to me. I owe them everything."

"You clearly mean the world to them, too." Kris pulled a paper and pen from his pocket and scribbled something. "Here's our phone number. Call or visit any time."

Lars lifted his eyebrows.

Marcie tucked the paper into a pocket. "I'd like that, but it might not be a good idea. My focus needs to be on helping them and facing whatever health problem Aunt Ingrid has. I don't want to set Uncle Halvor off again."

"It's nothing serious, I hope." The gentleness in Kris's tone nearly flooded her eyes.

"We're not sure. We should get answers today." She glanced at her watch. "I have to get to the clinic, and this line is long. I'd better leave and come back tomorrow."

"No. Move ahead of us." Kris waved her forward. "And I would like us to talk. I have ideas that might help both farms. If you see ways I can help, please tell me. If you don't think it's smart to come to our place, could we meet in town?"

"Maybe." She looked away. "It's just that Balsam is so small."

"It is. Would somewhere farther away be better?"

"Probably."

He snapped his fingers. "I know the place. I hear the new ice cream shoppe in Hudson is fabulous. If you ever go to Hudson, we can meet."

"People rave about that place. I do have to go to Hudson in two more days to get seedling test results."

"That's perfect. Give me your phone number, and we'll coordinate."

As she rattled it off, he jotted her number in the notebook from his jacket pocket.

"But I should phone you," she said. "It's safer that way."

She was finally first in line and bought three rolls of stamps. Kris turned to his dad. "Can you buy our stamps? I'll walk her out."

"Sure, son."

Lars took her place at the head of the line.

When Marcie reached the post office steps, it appeared Uncle Halvor was still asleep.

"I've enjoyed seeing you," Kris said. "I won't risk crossing the parking lot, but I hope you'll phone."

"No, you'd better not. But you will hear from me."

Returning to their truck, Marcie wondered if the threat of losing their farm fully explained all of Halvor's fury today. He'd been so out of control, Kris's dad could have pressed charges. How much was the pressure of Ingrid's undiagnosed illness? Or was Uncle Halvor getting ill himself?

She looked up to heaven for help. Halvor's actions did not match the kind uncle whose encouragement kept Mom and her afloat after someone T-boned Dad's car and killed him late one night. Dad's insurance had covered funeral expenses but little more. Not long after, mom got cancer. Thank God for Uncle Halvor and Aunt Ingrid. She would support them now as they had supported her then.

Marcie put on a fixed smile as she reentered the truck. She would do whatever it took to save Halvorsen Farms. And Ingrid would be fine. She had to be. The Lord wouldn't give them more than they could handle.

Without letting them know, she'd get up early tomorrow to conduct her own survey to see how many brown-tipped trees could be sufficiently trimmed free of blight to sell.

There had to be enough.

Lord, please help us. Don't let all the trees have blight. Kris and his family need help, too. They're good people.

Kris stood on the post office steps watching Marcie drive away. Why hadn't he stayed in touch?

Dad emerged with the stamps.

"She seems like a fine gal," Dad said as the Halvorsen truck turned the corner. "I hope he listens to her suggestions."

"Will he?"

"Hard to know. He resists change more than most of us. He's in debt so deep, I don't think even a complete overhaul can save him now."

"That bad?"

"Yup. We have rough times in beautiful Christmas tree land." Lars clapped Kris's shoulder. "C'mon, son. Let's head home."

"Sure. Do you mind if we stop a minute at the creamery on our way? They make the best cheese anywhere. There's nothing like it in New York. Grocery chain cheeses have little taste."

"Glad you noticed." His dad chuckled. "We do some things right in Balsam. But I hear our creamery's in trouble."

"You're kidding. Why?"

"They can't compete with big city prices."

"Probably don't charge enough for their great products."

"Maybe you should tell them."

"I'm not sure I should get involved."

"Our customers here are local folk, not gourmet buyers."

"True. Even if we educate the locals about its quality, they still might not have the money to pay higher prices. It's a vicious cycle."

The creamery door jingled as Kris and Lars entered. Kris busied himself choosing great cheese selections from the front shelves in the retail space as a man emerged from the back.

"Welcome," he called.

Kris did a double take when he saw his friend in white. "Dave? Dave Scholz?"

"Yeah. Great to see you, Kris."

They exchanged one-armed hugs.

"How are you, Dave? Dad, you remember my high school buddy?"

"Sure do. He asks about you whenever I come in."

Dave wiped his hands on his spotless apron. "We try to keep up with our town hero, Kris. Smalltown boy makes good in New York City. You work on the Rockefeller Plaza?"

Kris scuffed his feet. "Our offices are in a major building there, but I'm high up in a closet-sized space with a great view."

"That's still impressive."

"I guess." He laid his choices on the counter and reached for his billfold, but Dad beat him to it.

"I'll get it, son. But don't you want more?"

"Four pounds for two weeks? You'll faint when you see your grocery bill by the time I leave."

"We'll risk it."

"Check our new specialties," Dave said. "Besides our traditional curds and smoked flavors, we've combined green olives with chives and a brand-new jalapeño bacon cheddar. Next week we'll introduce a parsley, basil, garlic blend."

"Wow. Those all make my mouth water, but even I can't eat more in two weeks."

Dave offered a cheese tray. "Here, try these. If you can't eat more now, buy extra to take to the big city."

"That's a good idea, and these are great. I'll come back before I leave to stock up."

Dave lowered his tray. "I'll hold you to it."

"How's the creamery doing anyway?"

"Our customers love us and our recipes, but our financials don't show it. We need a stronger base. Since you're a financial advisor, you're someone we should talk to."

"I doubt that." Kris took a step back. "I'm a New York City think tank guy who generates ideas. They may not fit here."

Dave shook his head. "Good ideas work anywhere. We especially need tips on cost-efficient production and distribution. I'm thinking about creating a cheese-of-the-month club where subscribers sign up. Maybe also add a gift program. Or we could start a creamery co-operative that sells shares to the public and gives member discounts and dividends once things take off."

Kris nodded. "You've put thought into this. Co-ops work fine in real estate. They might work in food production. Let me think about it. I'd sign up for a monthly cheese program right now if you'd mail out the packages."

"Guaranteed!" Dave beamed. "Lisa and I are always hatching up new schemes. A good co-op could quick-start the development funds we need." He rang Kris's purchases into the cash register.

"Tell Lisa hi for me. How are you two, anyway?"

"Great. Marrying her was my best decision ever. She has a good job at the bank, and we're putting money aside. Another year and we might start building a house on her dad's land." He folded his hands together. "But major congratulations on your success story. Who would have thought you'd end up in New York City?

"Not me. That was not my original plan, but there aren't

enough opportunities here. People find them in the big city by working long, hard hours, but it's a rat race."

"I'll bet." One of Dave's eyebrows hiked. "That sounds like pressure to me. Life in Balsam must seem boring by comparison."

"No, just slower and different. Life there can be too exciting."

"I believe it. I read your headlines. Crazy traffic, gang fights, muggings. Here, boring means safe." He lifted a tray of cookies from underneath the counter. "Grab one. Lisa bakes these for sale and doesn't know I buy most of them to give our customers."

Kris bit into one. "Delicious. What are they?"

"Fresh snickerdoodles rolled in cinnamon and sugar."

"Fabulous. Add a dozen to our bill."

"Naw. I'm giving you these as a welcome home gift."

"Thanks, I appreciate that." Kris took another bite and handed a cookie to his dad.

"How long are you staying?" Dave asked.

"Two weeks."

"You should come by our place some evening."

"I'd like that."

"I'm glad you're doing well. You probably earn a fat paycheck."

Kris's tightened his lips. "Not fat, but I earn bonuses. Enough to see that hard work pays off."

Dad finished his cookie. "I wish working hard here raising Christmas trees or cheesemaking paid off. Maybe someday."

Kris paused. "That's why I'm here. I'd love to see things turn the right direction, even push forward."

"Forward?" Dave asked. "In Balsam?"

"It might be hard," Kris said, "but not impossible."

Lars paid and tucked the receipt in his wallet. "Kris has a good business head. He's thinking up ways we can streamline distribution."

Dave whistled. "That's what we need, too. Keep thinking big, Kris. You may find answers for all of us. Maybe you should run for mayor."

Kris shook his head. "No thanks."

"But if you stayed, we could watch you in action. Develop better business practices. Maybe start a *Rebuild Balsam* campaign."

"There's a thought, but you give me too much credit." Kris gave Dave a friendly jab. "If you're that keen, run for mayor yourself. The best leaders grow through on-the-job experience."

"So I've heard, but I'm more Junior Chamber of Commerce level."

"Naw. Jump into the big league. You'll find good mentors at county and state levels." Kris took another cookie. "Frankly, while you're at it, you and Lisa could start a bakery. These are fabulous."

"We've talked about it. She sells plenty to summer tourists and again at Christmas."

"I'll bet. We need a good bakery here. Maybe start a cookie mail-out club like the cheese idea." He dusted the crumbs from his hands. "For Christmas tree growing to be profitable, we need higher production on land here, but I don't see any more available. Halvorsen could do things to modernize his place, but I doubt he'd cooperate."

"You never know." Dave leaned against the counter. "He might have to work things out." He lowered his voice. "I think he's in trouble with the bank. He wouldn't voluntarily sell, but things are so tight, he needs a miracle."

Lars groaned. "I was afraid of that. Maybe that's why he was out of control today. He still hates me for buying half his land years ago, but more seems to be eating him now."

Dave hooked his thumbs into his apron ties. "Norway spruce blight is sinking him since that's mainly what he grows. Those were moneymakers years back, so that's most of what he put on all 320 acres. You have some blight, don't you, Lars?"

"A little, but not bad. Like most area growers, I diversified more, but we still have problems. Now that his niece is home, I hope she improves things for Halvor."

"She'd better be a miracle worker." Dave leaned against the counter. "You may have heard his wife is sick, too."

Lars paused. "I heard that rumor at church. Anything serious?"

"Can't say for sure. She's on the church prayer list as an unspoken request. The secretary slipped on the phone and said they're plenty worried."

"What a shame. I hope things turn out." Kris rested a hand on his dad's shoulder. "C'mon. We'd better head home before Mom sends out a search party."

"She might."

"Great seeing you, Kris. Do come by. Lisa would bake more cookies."

"Count me in." Kris flashed a grin.

After he and Dad climbed into the truck, Kris gripped the steering wheel a moment without turning the key.

"Dad? Do you think Halvorsen can make it?"

"I don't know, son. I hope so." Dad blew out air and gazed in the distance. "I hate to see anyone in foreclosure—not even my worst enemy, and Halvorsen isn't that."

"He's not?"

"Nope. He's unpleasant and annoying, so I stay out of his way, but I feel for him. He works harder than most guys I know. I hope he can survive whatever he's facing."

4

T he instant Marcie reentered the truck, her uncle's eyes snapped open.

"What took so long?"

"There was a long line."

"Hmmph."

As she drove through the parking lot, he leaned forward to peer through the window.

"That's Lundquist's truck. Was he in there?"

"Yes. It's the only post office in town. Everyone goes there."

"Did he bother you? Slow you down?"

"No. In fact, his son was helpful." She faced her uncle. "I'd still be in there if Kris hadn't had me step in front of them since I'm in a hurry. Lars knows Aunt Ingrid is sick. He wishes her and you well."

"That'll be the day." He snorted. "He fooled you, pulled the wool over your eyes. It tears me up that I'm struggling while he prospers on land that should be ours."

"He's not prospering that much. Apparently, Kris is home to help him with something."

"Isn't him stealing our land enough?"

"He bought it at auction when our family had to sell."

His head jerked. "Whose side are you on?"

"Yours, but I don't see sides. Our family needed a buyer, and the Lundquists bought. It's as simple as that."

"But he shouldn't keep it. Doesn't he know a man needs his family's land? It feels like I got my right arm cut off." He raised his. "I couldn't manage without this. The hardest part was Dad didn't tell Mom and me before he put up half our land for tax collateral and then lost it. First thing we knew, the bank printed auction bills and posted signs. We found out the hard way. Worst day of our lives. We could have been homeless."

He leveled a glance. "I hope you never experience anything like that. Dad considered shooting himself."

"Oh, no."

"He pulled his gun out but broke down and wept when Mom and I talked him out of it. All the same, I'll never forget the look on his face." Halvor shook himself as if to break free of bad memories. "He wasn't the same after that. He only lived another year before a stroke got him."

"That's awful. I didn't realize. Were you there at the auction?"

"Of course."

"Did many turn out?"

"You know small towns. They all did. Plus gawkers from other places. It was even advertised in the newspaper. I guess that's how Lundquist heard about it."

"So anyone with the top bid could have bought the land?"

"Yes, but did it have to be a stranger? And a Swede? As opposite to us Norskies as day from night."

"I'm thankful you didn't lose the whole place. The half you still own is beautiful. Besides, didn't God create both people?"

"I'm not sure. He loves Norskies best. And losing any land still hurts." He shuddered. "We have to find a cure for the blight, or I might have to sell more land. Maybe even the house. That's unthinkable."

He turned to stare out the window. "Frankly, I couldn't

survive that. I think I know how my dad felt. I'm Halvor Halvorsen, son of Halvor. In Old Norse, that means Guardian. I plan to fight for and guard this land if it kills me."

"Uncle Halvor, please don't talk that way." She rested a hand on his sleeve. "We'll find answers."

"Whether we do or not, here's the clinic. Let's hope your aunt has answers. And that it's better news, not worse."

Marcie wheeled into the parking area and spotted Aunt Ingrid standing in front of the clinic. Her aunt rushed to the truck with an unreadable facial expression.

"I thought you'd never get here," she panted. She massaged a shoulder and shifted her purse to her other side.

"What do you mean?" Halvor asked as he climbed out and hugged her. "This is when you said to come."

"The doctor wrapped up things a little faster than we thought."

"That sounds good," Marcie said. "Wait, Uncle Halvor. Don't get in the back. I'll ride there while you drive, so you'll both be up front together."

Ingrid smiled. "Thanks, dear. That's nice."

Marcie shifted the truck into park and got out.

Halvor gave Ingrid another hug before helping her into the passenger side.

"What did the doctor say?" he asked, hunching his shoulders as if preparing for bad news. "Wait, I'll pull to the side and park. I shouldn't be driving while you tell us."

"It's not that bad." But Ingrid looked hollowed out—tired and pale. Uncle Halvor looked almost the same.

"It's mostly fixable," she said. "I'll need your help changing life habits."

"Guaranteed," Halvor said. "We'll do anything."

"But what did the doctor say?" Marcie insisted.

"It's not terrible. There are guidelines, but my health isn't as bad as he thought."

"But what did he think, Ingrid Rose?" Uncle Halvor's face

purpled. Air whooshed from his lungs. He gripped the steering wheel so tight it squeaked. "Ingrid, tell us before my heart fails."

"I'm sorry, I'm mixed up inside. The biopsy he sent in is benign. Today's endoscopy nearly killed me but showed what's wrong. I should live to be an old lady."

She attempted a laugh which came out like a sputter.

Hands still clamped on the steering wheel, Uncle Halvor's purple face turned livid. "Ingrid, you're killing me. Give us plain talk!"

"I'm trying." Her face alternated between agony and relief. "After being so scared for so long, my emotions are a mess. Now that I know I'm not going to die like Marcie's poor mom, I just … I just …"

"Just what?"

Ingrid began to laugh uncontrollably. The more she tried to stop, the more she lost control. "Sorry, I'm so relieved," she gasped.

Uncle Halvor stared as if he'd never seen this woman before. "Ingrid, what's happening in that head of yours?"

"I don't know." Tears flooded her face as she fought for breath. "I can't help it. I thought I was dying, but I'm not." She clutched his arm and gasped. "Please understand, I'm just happy!"

She doubled over, whooping as Halvor shook his head and turned to Marcie.

"I give up. Can you do anything to calm her?"

"I don't know. Aunt Ingrid? Here's a thermos of water. Will that help?"

"Oh, my, yes. I'm dry as a bone. Laughed myself silly, I guess."

So weak she could barely hold the cup Marcie gave her, she gulped it down and hiccupped for more. She accepted a second cup and swallowed that, too.

When she finally calmed, Halvor took a long slow breath himself. "Now, tell us what your doctor said."

"He said … I forget the term, some fancy ulcer name. It's

printed on a report in my purse, but I needed out of the clinic. I'm supposed to drink lots of milk, like a baby. And eat bland food. And avoid stress."

When she said those last words, she hooted with laughter again.

"Avoid stress?" Halvor asked, his forehead rising. "He knows our tree growing troubles and said that? What's wrong with him?"

"I don't know ..." her words trailed off into more giggles.

The corner of Halvor's mouth tugged, and he gave up. With the truck still parked, he raised his hands from the steering wheel and threw back his head, joining in with small hoots that advanced to full-scale snorts. Marcie also finally succumbed, wiping her eyes and chuckling in the back seat.

After minutes of helpless hilarity, until they were weak but more at peace, Halvor started the engine, depressed the clutch, and shifted his truck into gear.

"Let's head home, even if we are all crazy." He still smiled more than Marcie had seen in days.

The rusty Halvorsen Farms truck clattered and banged its way through Balsam. It rolled along highway curves to the last hill on the Wisconsin side of the St. Croix River, where the sculpted bluffs on the Minnesota side became visible.

Drawing a deep breath, he stopped to enjoy his favorite overlook. This scenic river valley, with its evergreen-covered hills, was as lovely today as the hour the first Halvorsen arrived to stake out homestead land. Halvor breathed deeply again and refilled his lungs. Today, as on so many others, this view brought him peace. His roots here were as deep as the trees in his fields.

"We still have to fight our way out of a hard place," he said, a hint of hope warming his voice, "but we have a chance. If you'll stay healthy, my Ingrid, and with Marcie's help and God on our side, we have a chance to beat this problem."

"That's what I've been trying to tell you, Uncle Halvor," Marcie said. "Better days will come."

He entered their driveway, marked by a life-size color billboard of a Norway Spruce Christmas tree decorated with painted lights and garlands. During each November and December, real twinkling lights flashed from that tree sign and the two tall living trees defining both sides where the Halvorsens' driveway joined the road.

He let his engine idle while Marcie took mail from their box and handed it to him. He drove the remaining distance down the lane to their house and parked before checking the envelopes.

He raised his eyes from the mail to Ingrid. "Here's our light bill and weekly church news, plus something from the bank." He slid that envelope into his pocket. "I'll take care of that one in the morning after my new spark of courage has time to catch flame."

"Good," Ingrid sighed. "Please help me inside. It's been a fine day, but after so much good news, I'm suddenly worn out."

"Please go rest," Marcie said. "I'll fix dinner."

"Thanks. I wouldn't let you, but I need to stretch out. I'm not hungry, but if there's any baked custard left, that and maybe a piece of toast would hit the spot."

Marcie nodded. "I'll bring it to your room. What can I get you, Uncle Halvor?"

"I don't need to eat. Good news after so much bad perks me up better than food, and seeing those Christmas trees and sunset colors shining up there fixes up a fellow just fine."

"You need to eat, though. We have lots of hard work to do tomorrow. Plus, I'd like to ask you some farm questions. And have you consider some of my ideas."

"That's workable." He laid the mail on the sideboard in the dining room and sank into a chair by the window.

Marcie leaned forward to mimic a waitress writing orders on an order pad. "What would you like from our Halvorsen Farms Restaurant? Tonight's feature is grilled cheese sandwiches with homemade tomato soup. Or our pancake and egg scrambled plate called 'breakfast for dinner.'"

His blue eyes glinted with more joy than usual.

"Both sound good, but since I'm Norwegian and a Wisconsin cheese head, I'd take grilled cheese and soup, please. Two sandwiches, if it's okay."

"Good idea."

"When it's ready, may I eat here to enjoy the rest of this glorious sunset?"

"Yes, indeed. And I'll pull up a chair to join you."

5

Rounding the last curve, Kris loved seeing the full-size Lundquist Christmas Trees Farm sign he and Mom had crafted several Christmases ago. Santa's large, loaded sleigh was visible to all drivers approaching the St. Croix River overlook near their driveway opposite the Halvorsen's. The wording below read *Sleigh Rides, Gifts, Cut your own tree—Make this your farm for a day*!

Their efforts turned out well. Area schools came for field trips. By spending a little more energy, Kris knew they could invite schools and organizations throughout Wisconsin, Minnesota, Iowa, and beyond. He had developed a colorful display showing the tree growth cycle from cone gathering seeds to final harvest. He should check with Marcie to make sure his terms were right. She was the expert.

As soon as their Ford F-100 turned into the lane and Dad grabbed the mail from their box, Kris saw a golden streak race down the driveway as his dog welcomed him home.

"How does he do that?" Kris asked, hopping out as his golden lab, Marmaduke, hurtled into his arms and licked him thoroughly.

"Not sure. Maybe a combination of things," Dad said. "He

senses our excitement and probably also smells you. He's so much part of our family, I think he understands our conversations. Probably heard your name. He *always* knows what's going on."

"Tell me about it." Kris buried his face in Duke's fur, arms tight around his neck until the dog wriggled free to lick him thoroughly again.

"I'm not licking back, buddy. I draw the line there." Kris relaxed as the comfortable reality of being back home bubbled up inside.

"It's about time you got here," Mom called from the porch, letting the door bang shut behind her. "You must have flown on an antique prop plane instead of a jet."

Her apron flapped cheerfully, and she held a wooden spoon as she also crossed the driveway. They met halfway.

"Everything just took longer than I figured."

"I've missed you." She reached up to gather him in her arms. "I promise not to cry, but then I always do."

"It's okay. Mom, you look great!" He squeezed her back, kissing her cheek. "Mmmm, you smell like apple pie, roast beef, and fresh yeast rolls."

"You're good. That's our menu. How did you know?"

"You always fix my favorites when I come home."

They threw back their heads and laughed.

"I've got your bag, son." Dad set it on the porch. "We'll unload my hardware supplies later. Let's go inside."

"It's not every day our famous son returns for a visit." Mom stood on tiptoe and kissed his cheek again.

"Uh, you shouldn't do that. Duke got me first."

"That rascal. He always finds you first. Hearing him bark is how I knew you were finally here." She hugged Kris again. "Come on in. I cooked up a storm. Everything is ready."

Kris sighed with contentment. "Mom, really. Having you go all out is why I wanted to surprise you so you wouldn't do all this."

"What?" She stiffened and stretched to full height, raising her wooden spoon like a battle weapon. "And rob me of welcoming you home like I want?"

"If you put it that way. I just hate seeing you work so hard."

"It's not work if I enjoy it."

"Give up and listen to her, son. You won't win."

Lars pulled his wife and Kris into a three-way hug.

"She's right. It's great having our loved ones within arm's reach." His eyes moistened. "Thank you, Lord. A man lives for days like this."

6

I t stormed overnight at Halvorson Farms. Clouds piled high on top of each other until squeezing out enough rain to make things clean and fresh before moving on.

Marcie had laid out breakfast things the night before. Long before time to start pancake batter or fry bacon, when the sun barely edged the horizon, she slipped outside to get a look at the spruce blight damage. On their way home that first night, Uncle Halvor had stopped the truck to show her some of the worst of it, but she'd been so distracted by seeing how the worry was aging him, she'd focused on him more than the blighted trees.

She drew in a deep spruce-scented breath. This was her favorite time of day. Dad had grown up on his own, without having or knowing much family. After his tragic death, Marcie legally accepted Mom's maiden name Halvorsen as her own, with Dad's name in the middle.

She must be Norwegian all right, somewhere in family history, because she'd also be content to live in this beautiful place forever and make it more productive.

At university, she'd studied healthy trees versus diseased conditions until she knew the stages and could easily spot warning signs. It was easiest to learn what healthy trees looked like and then notice the difference. Silviculturists researchers were making more discoveries every day, but eradication and treatment depended on the type of problem and its cause.

This morning's search confirmed that many tree tips had turned brown and were curling. Many new growth buds were brown and brittle. She fanned the needles, checking for pests or cankers underneath but found none. That was good news. Yet the trees looked so bad, it was depressing. She racked her brain. Could anything she'd learned show a way to save them? She'd do her best to salvage all she could for sale.

Thankfully, she'd brought her textbooks home. Here, she quickly found what she needed. Uncle Halvor understood most of the details. She would condense the scientific terms to more basic ones for Aunt Ingrid, but she had a good understanding, too. The culprit was either a fungus or pest.

The best article explained both causes well. Her research indicated it might be a fungus that wintered in infected shoots, bark, and/or cones. From spring to fall, the spores were abundant when the new shoots, or candles, formed. After opening, the shoots couldn't be infected. Wind and rain spread the fungus. If spores reached susceptible trees, they penetrated open wounds and spread through stems into needles and cones. Then the needles turned brown and died quickly.

There was so much information. How much should she pass on? She fanned branches near the top of each tree and knelt to the base of their trunks. When candles were weak, brittle, and broke easily, it was likely a shoot-borer insect instead.

Marcie sighed with relief. Everything she saw looked like fungus, easier to treat than conifer borers and flying moths. Her hands-on experience here was as valuable as her university lab studies. She'd draw out Uncle Halvor to hear what he knew already and then add university updates where they fit. He'd been as loving and wonderfully supportive of her as she remembered her Dad being. But Halvor was such a proud

Norwegian. Would he find it hard to learn from a girl? Even one graduating as a silviculture specialist?

Lord, keep him encouraged while we work through our problems. You're the Creator and world's best problem-solver. Help us see Your answers.

By the time she returned to the house, he was up and had started his powerful coffee.

"Out for a morning stroll?" he asked.

"Yes. It's beautiful out. Mist rising from the river valley with the sun coming up is as beautiful as the Japanese scroll paintings in Madison's art museum. I'll bring my camera next time."

His face looked more relaxed.

"I'm glad to say your aunt slept well, and her color seems better. She says she's ready for morning coffee, though."

Marcie froze. "Should she drink that with an ulcer?"

"Probably not. Maybe with lots of milk poured in to dilute it. I doubt we'll change her overnight—she's also Norwegian."

He chuckled and carried Ingrid a cup of pale milky coffee.

After their hearty breakfast, Halvor and Marcie piled into the truck to go to the farthest rows of trees overlooking the river.

"By taking the pick-up, we'll have tools along to prune branch tips, collect samples, or anything we need. It's easier than carrying them."

"For sure." Marcie removed her work jacket and left it in the truck since the day was already heating up.

Halvor kept his on. He unfolded his map of field plots showing where trees were planted by years and groups. The dates and tree variety were also flagged with color-coded squares of cloth wired to each tree. Most were Norwegian spruce, so their gold squares waved in the breeze.

Marcie carried notes in a clipboard and her best plant pathology book. "I also brought a thermos of coffee plus a jug of cold water for us. We'll work up a thirst in no time."

"Smart girl."

Bouncing along the dirt track between rows brought them through the heart of the remaining three hundred and twenty acres. The trees had been planted and placed well originally and then thinned and pruned into perfect conical shapes. As she and Halvor reached the property boundary above the beautiful, flowing river, they left the truck to gaze sadly at severe cases of Norway spruce blight.

"These trees are ten years old, almost ready for harvest." Halvor stretched tall to measure himself against them. "Most folks want seven-foot trees in their homes. These were as green as grass, well-shaped, and doing great, but now look at their tips. This just happened in the last few weeks."

Marcie nodded. "It's sad. From my plant pathology book, it looks like a fungus. It matches pictures of ruined trees with their growth tips turned brown and curling."

"But what causes it? Years have gone by with no problem. And then, in a tight year financially, it suddenly hits. It reminds me of the book of Job."

"I don't think I'd go that far," Marcie said. "The Lord is with us, and we'll find answers."

Insects rose and buzzed in the mid-day heat. Halvor and Marcie briefly stepped inside the red packaging and shipping shed for cooling shade.

Halvor waved a hand. "Ingrid's done her part. She ordered ahead when prices were good to have most of the twine, tags, labels, and netting on hand for us. Now, we just need nice big Christmas orders and healthy trees to ship."

"It will happen, Uncle Halvor. I'm not sure how, but I believe it will."

"I hope you're right."

They went outside again, checking, measuring, taking photographs, and collecting samples until mid-afternoon. They knew the condition of the first half of their trees.

"We need a break," Halvor said. "We should put something in our bellies before we faint in this heat."

"I'm sorry. I should have planned better and started something in the slow cooker. I'm preoccupied with the trees."

"Me too, and it's fine."

Hot and tired, they returned to the farmyard with its welcoming house in its center. *It needs freshening up, too,* Marcie thought. *A new coat of paint would do wonders for this shed. It shouldn't cost that much. I wonder if I could pull off a surprise ...*

She and Halvor kicked off their boots on the porch and entered the comfortable old farmhouse. Delicious smells curled from the kitchen and pulled them in.

"What's going on?" Uncle Halvor whipped his head around. "Ingrid, what are you up to?"

His wife stood in the kitchen doorway, face wreathed in smiles. Her gray-blonde hair was pulled back from her face and showed cheeks much rosier than yesterday and brighter from cooking over the hot kitchen range.

"What am I up to? Five foot six inches last I checked. Having fun, and you two came right on time. I was about to ring the dinner bell. I figured you'd be half-starved by now."

Halvor pulled her into a hug and reached his other arm out for Marcie.

"This is the way life is meant to be. It's so good having you back home, Marcie, and not just to help with the trees. We miss you something fierce when you're not here. Now our house has its soul again."

"Uncle Halvor, that's a sweet thing to say."

"You know it's true!"

She sighed with contentment. "Balsam is where I want to be."

"That's good to hear." Ingrid's dimples flashed. "We were afraid Madison might tempt you or perhaps some handsome young man there."

"Frankly, I met more frogs than princes."

"But did you kiss them to find out?" Her aunt's dimples flashed. Marcie made a face at her aunt but laughed.

After washing up, Halvor and Marcie returned to the table.

"Aunt Ingrid, you've worn yourself out again. Meatloaf and mashed potatoes—my favorites."

"I'm not worn out when I'm doing what I like. More of your favorites, too. Halvor, please carry this bowl to the table."

"Gladly." A happy smile lit his gaunt face.

"Marcie. If you'll bring this platter, I'll bring the milk pitcher myself."

"You fixed this feast for us?" Marcie asked. "What's here that you can eat?"

"A few things. It's okay." Ingrid's eyes sparkled. "I added enough milk to the mashed potatoes to make a good soup. It's so tasty, you'll beg for some yourself. I figure the faster I cooperate, the sooner I'll be normal again. I plan to heal just fine." She cocked her head at a perky angle.

"That is such good news, my Ingrid."

After pulling out chairs for his wife and Marcie, Halvor clasped his hands. "This is another fine meal to thank our Lord for."

Ingrid beamed. "Then ask the blessing, and we'll start."

They joined hands, and he bent his head. "Gracious Heavenly Father, thank You for these wonderful gifts—my wife's good cooking and Marcie being home. You are always good. I know you'll give us answers about the trees. Bless this food to our bodies and us to Your service. Amen."

"How did you find things outside?" Ingrid asked.

"Not wonderful, but it could be worse," he said. "I'm so starved, and this tastes so good, I'd like to eat first and then explain."

When his eating slowed, he pushed back. "Ah, Ingrid. Am I ever thankful I found you years ago. Every single thing hit the spot. You'll win blue ribbons at the county fair again this year."

"Well, it's usually me or Karin Lundquist. Two farm wives who love cooking."

"Both sweethearts. No complaints about that," Marcie said.

Halvor took a last swallow of milk and wiped his mouth. "Now, here's our farm situation. The trees least affected are the oldest stand of original trees downhill toward the river that were already growing when the first Halvorsen homesteaded here. I don't know if someone else had planted them or they were somehow volunteer."

"That's interesting. Could that happen?" Ingrid asked.

"Sometimes. Those beauties gave him the idea of starting a Christmas tree farm. The other stand of good trees is the corridor of giants that starts at our driveway, but those are mixed trees—even some balsam fir and a few pine."

"I'm thankful to have any trees without blight."

"Yes," Marcie said. "The ones unaffected are some of our biggest, best trees. I'll check them carefully and take more pictures. I'm in touch with my Madison advisor, maybe we can figure out if there's something different about the soil there. Or better drainage, or any factor we can find."

Marcie buttered a piece of bread and spread her favorite homemade raspberry jam on it.

"Uncle Halvor? Remember the hundred experimental baby spruce seedlings I sent you six months back? Did you get those started?"

He looked down a moment before facing her. "It's too soon to tell." And then he gulped. "I should tell the truth. It's hard for me to accept new things, so I didn't give them a very serious try. I stuck them in the ground, but when I got busy, I had the schoolboy down the road take over when he comes for Saturday chores. I haven't looked at them since. I guess we should."

"Yes. I want to check them here compared to our regular nursery plants. I'll do the hard stuff—keep records, do comparison checks. And I have more ideas." She rattled a few off in fairly complex silviculture terms.

Halvor smiled. "You know, change isn't as hard when you're talking to me." He eased his shoulders.

"I'm glad. My advisor's guidance has helped me lots. He's up-to-date on strategies with proven results."

His smile broadened. "I guess that means sometimes change is good."

She grinned back. "I think so. We'll work together until we find answers to get through this."

"You betcha."

Marcie stared. "Uncle Halvor, you really do sound Norwegian."

When they finished the meal, Ingrid stood and started stacking dishes until Marcie stopped her.

"That was wonderful, but you're not doing dishes. Remember the rule Mom and I had? Cooks don't clean up. I thought you agreed on that, too."

"Usually." Ingrid fluttered a hand. "But I'm feeling so much better, I'm glad to work here while you two do outside work. I don't have that much energy back yet."

"But you will," Halvor said. "Thank God for your improvement. All the same, don't use it all up at once and then crash."

"I won't, and I'm listening." She planted a kiss on his weathered cheek and settled back in her chair, watching her niece put things away.

"Marcie, you amaze me. Even after being gone most of this year, you come home and remember where every plate, cup, and bowl goes."

"That's because it's my kitchen, too, and memories stick. Unless you change things like where you hide chocolate chips to keep them from Halvor."

"What's this?" He'd been scanning a state tree growers report, but his head jerked up. "A conspiracy against me?"

The ladies laughed.

Marcie stored the food in Tupperware containers and swished her way through the dishes. "Do you want our leftovers in the refrigerator or the freezer?"

"The fridge, please. We'll finish them off tomorrow and then choose new recipes to try. As much as I love to cook, it gets old fixing the same dishes for the same two people. Let's you and I find new ones to branch out."

"And find tasty things for your diet restrictions, too."

"Just don't forget Christmas lutefisk and lefse," Halvor said. "Don't get too newfangled."

"We'd never do that," Ingrid said.

Marcie wrinkled her nose. "I'm not full Norwegian, then. I can't stand lutefisk."

"If liking that defines true Norwegians, there can't be many around," Ingrid said. "I can't stand the way lutefisk makes our fridge smell, but lefse is fun to make."

"And eat." Halvor put down his tree growers report and tried to hide his smile. "What's this traitorous talk under our roof? There aren't better things to eat than lutefisk and lefse, but I'll let you try a few new recipes. Let's head to the shipping shed. I'm thinking about putting on a small addition where you could start seedlings from cones if you like. With your education, you could grow enough for us and extra for cash. Maybe even develop new varieties. What do you think?"

Marcie stared at him for a moment. "I think you're amazing to consider new ideas." She hugged him. "That especially makes me happy because it fits my training so well. I'd love my education to help our farm plus bring in income. Talk to me more about that as we check the remaining trees."

"Sure. We'll let our ideas percolate and see where they take us." He opened the door and let Marcie step out first.

"We won't be long, Ingrid. Please rest," he said. "Later, if you want to look at that home repair list again of things you'd like done, it's easier for me to catch up with Marcie home. I think most of your ideas need more elbow grease than money."

"That's true, and that's a good thing." She raised smiling eyes. "And you're right, they mostly need elbow grease. You've had so much on your mind, I didn't want to bother you, but it pleases me you remembered." She stepped to her antique sideboard and picked up a tablet with a few items listed.

"You're welcome. That's the least I can do for my bride." Their tender look was an embrace.

One day Marcie hoped for a marriage like theirs. Halvor and Ingrid had been through many troubles, but their deep love held them close.

Marcie joined Halvor in the truck and this time they parked near the faded red processing shed to check the trees beyond it. He had last painted the shed the same year Marcie and her mom arrived. Somehow repainting it hadn't been high enough on the priority list since. He and Ingrid had paid Marcie's first-semester university and dorm fees. By the second semester, she'd begun earning work-study grant money.

The shed's exterior color had faded. Alternating freezing and thawing weather had also made the wood crack and chip.

"Wow. It looks like it needs tender care soon, or we might be facing drastic repairs."

"I can't buy the paint this season, though," Halvor said. "That has to wait. We have bigger priorities. But I have recycled lumber that could build an addition."

"Maybe. The shed needs serious maintenance, though, or we'll lose it. I'll see if I can come up with anything."

Halvor opened the shed's creaking door for Marcie to enter. One look confirmed he'd been stretched far too thin to take care of the worse problems inside. The ceiling was festooned with thick ropes of spider webs spooky enough for a Halloween event. Worse, ant trails and sawdust where the floor joined outside walls showed places where the foundations must be rotting.

She occasionally earned extra money tutoring. When she talked to Madison next, she'd see if there were any students she could work with by phone. There had to be ways to make a difference.

Her uncle pulled two square hay bales together to make

room for them to sit. He'd hauled several inside for customer seating when he and Ingrid hosted Christmas events here in the past but hadn't had the energy to continue that for a while.

Aunt Ingrid had talent with food and crafts, and Halvor was knowledgeable in tree farming. Less skilled in socializing. When he hadn't been re-elected President of the local Chamber of Commerce, it hit him hard. He'd served the Mid-west Tree Growers board for years, too, before that stopped.

Stress combined with aging was hard. Was he declining? Marcie's brain kicked into high gear. She'd better pay closer attention and talk him into a medical check-up soon.

He noticed her preoccupation.

"What's bothering you, Marcie?" he asked, his tone kind.

She gazed into his lake-blue eyes, so much like Mom's.

"I'm almost glad you need help now so I can show how thankful I am for how you helped Mom and me. You're family."

He lifted his chin and scratched his neck. "For sure. Always have been, always will be."

"If you hadn't helped in her last year." Marcie shuddered. "It would have been so much worse."

"But we did. She was my sister. We would have felt awful if she hadn't let us." He patted her shoulder. "We love you, Marcie. Our business was solid then. By the time it wasn't, you had landed work-study programs. Later, we might not have managed as well." His Adam's apple bobbed. "You make us proud. And bring us joy."

Marcie choked up with a tender ache inside. She wouldn't only keep telling Ingrid and Halvor thanks. She would find more ways to show it. She swallowed twice, working to regain composure.

"When we needed help, you stepped in. Losing Dad crushed Mom. Before long, she got the cancer diagnosis. I'm sure those events are connected."

"I suspect you're right."

She looked him in the eye. "Did you know what you were getting into, taking on a dying woman and her young kid?"

"No one ever foresees everything. She was my sister, and you're my niece—but you're so much more to us now." His face softened. "The hardest part was at first when she wouldn't agree to come."

"She was numb. She didn't know what she wanted."

"And wouldn't accept help from anyone until she finally believed we truly wanted you both. We were so glad when you finally came. We've had sad times, but wonderful ones, too."

"That's nice of you to say since there was so much. I can never thank you enough."

He bristled. "Please stop thanking us. It was the right choice, but we also benefitted."

"Changing locations did help her move past part of the grief." Marcie shifted and pulled a hay stem from the bale she sat on, breathed in its sweetness, and stuck it in her mouth to chew. "Now, I almost can't remember not living here. I sure can't do this in Madison."

Halvor pulled out his own hay stem to stick in his mouth and chew. "If you don't watch out, in no time you'll be a grassroots farmer like me with hayseeds in your hair. Say, have I told you my latest Sven and Ole joke yet?"

"I don't think so. Maybe save it for dinner so Aunt Ingrid can hear, too."

"I could tell it twice."

He lifted his eyebrows and looked so hopeful, Marcie cocked her head to give him closer scrutiny. He was definitely trying to make her laugh.

"Nice try, Uncle Halvor. Are you trying to cheer me up?"

"Maybe." His grin widened. "Is it working?"

"Almost." He drove her crazy sometimes with his corny jokes, but maybe they were comic relief to lighten his farm concerns plus Ingrid's health. Had she gone too far rattling off endless academic silviculture terminology? He had years of hands-on tree-growing experience, just not all the technical terms. She needed to affirm him more, give him more credit.

He studied his stubbed fingertips briefly and uncrossed his legs before standing and pulling her into an awkward hug.

"You're our best girl. You've been through a bunch. So have we, but we're all good together. We can't imagine life without you and don't want to. We're so glad you came."

His tenderness unraveled her. The lump in her throat swelled so big she couldn't handle it, and she sniffed and dripped on his stooped shoulder. He smelled like her favorite things—fresh earth, and spruce trees, and honest sweat. He was such a good man.

He hemmed and hawed while trying to dry her tears.

"It's okay, Marcie. Let it out so you'll feel better. We've got all day."

That made her laugh out loud. They both knew they didn't have all day, but she rested a moment longer in his arms.

When he hauled out his red print farm handkerchief, she blew and honked almost as loudly as he was famous for.

"Thanks." She handed it back.

"If it's okay with you, let's tell your aunt the easy version of our tree problems, not scary details. We'll just say we need more prayer, which is always true." He searched her eyes. "Okay?"

"Okay."

"I don't want her worried more than she has to be. I want her well." He waved his arm toward their fields outside. "Besides, even with the answers we don't know, all of this isn't too big for God."

Marcie tipped her head back and smiled. "Couldn't say it better myself."

7

———————

When she and Mom had come here to stay, Halvor and Ingrid did wonders to make their home welcoming. At first, they hadn't known it was cancer, but because Mom hadn't been feeling great, they established her on the main floor. Her room had cream walls with a border of pale lilacs so real you could almost smell their fragrance. They kept her room full of fresh bouquets and lovely dried arrangements when flowers didn't bloom outside. They deserved top prize for making Mom's last year beautiful. It eased Marcie's heart to remember.

"It's too much!" Mom often said.

"Nope. Enjoy it. Only the best for my sister. We're so glad you two are here." Their actions showed it.

As for Marcie, they had completely redone a bedroom for a lively nine-year-old they didn't yet know very well.

She squealed when the door opened and she saw the Cinderella theme.

"Is this mine? You did this for me?"

Her aunt and uncle beamed. "We sure did, kiddo."

Mom teared up. "It's perfect. How did you know she would love this?"

"It wasn't hard," Ingrid said. "Last Christmas, we were

49

looking through a catalog together, and she showed me a Cinderella dress she was saving for. That gave me the idea."

"You did great," Mom said.

Marcie jumped up and down and threw herself across the hand-sewn white coverlet with birds embroidered in each corner.

"But where did you get the stuff?" Mom asked. "I wouldn't know where to find these things, not even in Madison. Like the curtains!"

"It took a while," Ingrid said, "but if you know what you need and keep looking in shops and catalogs, things usually turn up. I found yard goods on a discontinued print sale in a fabric store and whipped up the curtains. These things were meant for Marcie."

A colorful hand-braided rug brightened the floor by the refinished maple bed frame and dresser that looked similar to the set Uncle Halvor had stored in the barn.

Cinderella danced at the ball on every panel of the beautiful curtains while the handsome prince offered a sparkling glass slipper along the print's lower border.

"It's all wonderful. She'll never forget."

And she hadn't. Marcie loved the room so much, she kept it the same long past when her Disney phase ended, only adapting it a little in her teenage years with colors that reflected her love of the summer fields and things growing outside. She had hated leaving her sanctuary, even to go to school, and she was glad to be home from university to stay.

Halvor and Ingrid had picked her up from the bus coming from Madison. They helped carry her luggage but waited at her closed bedroom door while she climbed the stairs.

Their smiles tipped her off that something was different. She opened the door and saw that Aunt Ingrid had transformed her room once more.

Despite short finances, accent pillows in luscious sherbet colors highlighted the bed and chair. They'd added a larger refinished desk and brass lamp, and cream valances over the windows framed a view of the Christmas tree rows and distant hills.

"I'm too old now for you to keep spoiling me," she said. "You have too much on your plates." But then she sprawled across the simple new coverlet Ingrid had sewn, laughing for joy. "But I'm so glad you did!"

"Nothing cost much," Ingrid waved a hand. "I know how to find a bargain. We wanted to do it, so we found ways."

"It's so nice having you home!" Halvor beamed.

Although she'd outgrown the Cinderella theme years ago, the room still felt special.

"You keep filling this room with love," Marcie said and flung her arms around them.

Because of this kindness and so many, Marcie would make sure their older years were special. She just hoped she wasn't starting too late.

She and Halvor would solve the Christmas tree problems, and Ingrid would get well. She had to.

The next morning, the first light of dawn was Marcie's alarm clock. She started early to surprise her aunt and uncle with Swedish pancakes: light, fluffy, silver-dollar size disks slathered in butter and lingonberry jam she'd splurged on from the import store near campus.

"Swedish pancakes, you say?" Uncle Hal had asked, smiling, while filling his plate a second time. "You sure these tasty things aren't *Norwegian* pancakes?"

Lifting the next batch from the pan, she said, "It's okay if you prefer to call them that, but I think you exaggerate loving Norwegian things to get a rise out of people."

He exhaled loudly. "Would I do that?"

"You certainly would. All your talk about wanting a Norwegian Elkhound, Norwegian Fjord horses, troll garden figures, and anything Norwegian is overboard. Didn't I hear you praise Swedish Volvos?"

"Oops. I slipped. I admit, in cars, the Swedes set a high standard."

Aunt Ingrid rolled her eyes. "You tell him, Marcie. Rein him in before he gets worse and talks both your ears off instead of just one. He doesn't know when to stop."

But her blue eyes twinkled as she poured them second cups of coffee and gathered up plates.

He clasped his hands under a smug Cheshire cat expression.

"At least you're listening. You two can't tell if I'm serious or not. My ideas need more manpower than we have now, but it could happen." He gave a slow wink. "Wouldn't it be great to spotlight our Norwegian heritage? Introduce our homesteader pioneers? They deserve it. Make our barn area a Norwegian theme Santa Village with North Pole helpers? Of course, we could do lots more if we hadn't lost half our land."

"Halvor, it's okay." Ingrid ruffled his thinning gray hair as she passed behind his chair, returning a vase of purple asters to the table. "Don't fuss over spilled milk. We have plenty to keep us busy."

She reset the table for lunch now, placing silverware under plates, with cups and plates turned upside down to avoid flies while they did outside chores.

He stood and stretched and walked to the corner behind the door. "Has anyone seen my electric drill? I could have sworn I left it here. It's not in the shed either."

"Have you tried the basement?" Marcie asked. "Some things pile up there."

"Yup. Not there. If I don't find it, I'll buy a new one at the hardware tomorrow, bring it home and watch where I put it to find them both. Then, I can take the new one back for a refund." He cackled. "Just watch. It'll work."

"Are you serious?" Ingrid shook her head. "It probably will. Your stories grow like Pinocchio's nose, but I believe this one. I think you believe your stories yourself."

"I do." His eyes glinted as he put on his cap. "And they're good ideas. Just watch, they'll come true."

"We're too old for new plans, Halvor. It's time to think about slowing down and resting."

"We can't afford it yet. And speak for yourself. We're not that old. And with Marcie home ..." He glanced her way. "She's as full of vim and vigor as I was, as full of fight as a rooster seeing the ax. She'll improve our circumstances and help us regain our youth."

He poked Ingrid in the ribs, and she blushed.

"Don't get too full of plans, dear." Weariness slowed her words. "I've only been up two hours, but your talk about work is wearing me down today."

The banter left his voice. "What's wrong?"

"Nothing. I guess it takes a while to get all the way better. I'm ready for a nap."

"Please rest, sweetheart. Join us outside later if you want. Or stay inside. Marcie and I can do what's needed outside the rest of this morning." He flexed an arm. "We'll head out there and get our miracle rolling."

"That's a tall order, Uncle Halvor." Marcie rested a hand on his arm. "I'll do my best, but don't set your hopes too high or put more faith in me than I can make happen. Just because I've almost finished a silviculture degree doesn't mean I know everything." She flashed a grin. "Even if I act like it."

He chuckled. "That makes two of us."

"But your life experience and my head knowledge will work together."

"That's right." His smile faded. "I don't mean to pressure you, gal. We're going to hit our problems hard with our best shots, so my hopes shoot high like the man I used to be."

"You're still great. And you're a riot always praising Norwegian things. I don't think you're serious half the time." She filled a water jug for her backpack.

"Oh, ya. Half the time."

She added twine and tape to her backpack. And a magnifying glass. "You have some good ideas there. The Norwegian gift shops in Mt. Horeb near Madison have great small-town charm. Their bakery sells out every afternoon, and people keep their coffee shop full all day."

"Ingrid and I have mentioned that. Something similar could work in Balsam."

"But not for us to do, Halvor," Ingrid said. "For younger folks. And if our whole town worked together ..."

His eyes grew dreamy. "We're not that far from the Twin Cities. Or Hinckley, or Duluth, or Madison, or even Milwaukee. We could brainstorm with our tree growers and merchants to become a tourist destination town."

"Things like that work." Marcie's hands dropped to her hips. "But I can't believe my eyes and ears, Uncle Halvor. Are you becoming an idea man?"

"Maybe. Lots of thoughts stir in my head. Maybe it's fresh blood from you coming home. I won't be Chamber president much longer, but I can mention ideas. Maybe talk to the Regional Board. If I could get that hard-headed Lars Lundquist to hush up and listen—"

Ingrid stared. "Who's hard-headed? Two of them live across the road from each other."

"You're right." Marcie paused. "But I think Lars is willing to listen. He's just not sure how to implement things. But whether he is or not, you have good ideas. It would take leadership and money, but once people see possibilities, something could happen. Maybe even financial security. Take our farms and businesses to a whole new level. Really put Balsam on the map."

"Now you're talking!" Halvor slapped his Halvorsen Farms hat on his head.

"But Halvor, I'm concerned. Don't get your hopes high and be disappointed."

"I won't, Ingrid." He turned to Marcie. "What do you say, girl?"

"Most ideas sound impossible at first—horseless carriages, flying machines. But if God is giving you even half of these thoughts and Balsam's people work together, this could become a wonderful place."

He put his hand on the doorknob and blew his wife a kiss.

"See! What did I tell you? Our girl's got spunk."

"I know where she gets it," his bride said kindly. "Now, if you can dredge up enough energy to match, you'll accomplish something." She turned to Marcie. "I've got lunch covered. I'll heat leftovers when it's time."

"Thanks. Everything tasted so great last night, it'll be even better today." She grabbed Uncle Halvor's worn tan Carhartt jacket from its peg near the door to wear until she could buy her own. Except she'd choose forest green. "Besides, there's nothing better than your cooking anywhere."

8

The spruce blight damage had advanced from two nights ago. Uncle Halvor had stopped the truck that night to show her the damage up close as they drove in from town.

"It's worse than I expected," she'd said, brow puckered.

"At first, I thought I was my imagination. Maybe how morning light hit or how afternoon sunshine slanted on the branches, but soon it was obvious. And getting worse each day." He took a few steps. "But look here. A few younger trees look blight-free. Why? What's different? Is it the soil? Something in the stock they're from?"

"We have to find out. We can prune and shape the damaged trees, I think," Marcie said. "And for sure trim tip damage from the less infected ones, so they're good enough to sell. They should be fine."

Uncle Halvor lifted his hat and ran his hand through his thinning hair. "I don't know, Marcie. What if the brown advances more once we've trimmed the trees? What then? My customers would hit the roof. We'd lose our business."

"We have to try something. Let's trim a few and see how they look. Try these new pruners." She clacked the pruning shear blade edges together. "Cut off the growth tips, and I think they'll be passable for sale. Unless they still shed like Charlie Brown's Christmas tree."

He shuddered. "Don't even say that. Let's try."

"I'm keeping track of each one." She removed a notepad and pencil from her slacks pocket. "How come some trees are okay? Especially that tall stand of original trees near the river—what makes them free of blight? If we can solve that, we can start turning things around. It's time to do a soil analysis on several plots."

His face had a new shine. "Darned if you don't make me feel hopeful."

"Good, that's my goal." She looked at her watch. "Time is flying. I'm going to examine those resistant trees now. More needles for analysis, take more pictures. It looks like there's more gravel in soil under our best trees. Maybe that helps soil filtration."

He scrunched his forehead.

"I appreciate your help. Tell me as soon as you even guess what's going on."

9

Hudson's ice cream shoppe wasn't fancy by New York City standards, but it was perfect in Wisconsin. Kris arrived ten minutes early just in case. Today he wore the new blue shirt Mom had sent for his birthday that highlighted his eyes. He had scored the last seats in the place, a cute table for two near the back. Marcie walked in, craning her neck to find him until he stood.

"Marcie. Over here."

He enjoyed her smile as he seated her. Heads turned as she came in. Wow, she looked swell. Instead of green slacks today, she wore a white dress with capped sleeves and red polka dots that matched the shoppe's décor.

"You're wearing the right colors," he said. "Black and white floor tiles, red and white vinyl booths, and shiny chrome counter."

"I guess I do match."

"I'll give the soda jerk our order after you see the menu. You should be on its cover."

She partially hid the shy flush of her cheeks by raising her menu to read.

"I'm eager to try something."

She settled on a bubbly cherry phosphate while he chose a double chocolate malt.

"I need more reasons to come to Hudson," Kris said, "or hope they build one in Balsam."

"That's a great idea—if we grow big enough to sustain it."

"You came for seedling test results today. How did those turn out?"

"Pretty well, thanks. I can't wait to pass the information on to my research advisor in Madison. We're working to develop seedlings that will produce tall, strong timber that's more resistant to pests and fungi."

"Amazing." He raised his eyebrows. "That would be any tree grower's dream. If you did all that, the whole silviculture industry should award you top prize."

"Nothing happens overnight, but we're seeing gains. I'm excited to mail him some growth tip needles and seed cone samples."

Kris paused. "I might be sitting with a young woman who will become famous in the tree-growing industry."

Her cheeks pinked. "I don't want to be famous. I just want to help area growers find ways out of the difficult places we've been in."

"That may be the clearest action statement I've heard in months."

When their delicious concoctions reached the table, they both took long appreciative sips.

"Look at the pile of whip cream on mine," Kris said. "Yours looks less decadent."

"It's perfect," she said. "Girls appreciate fewer calories."

"You'll never need to worry," he said appreciatively and saw more color rise to her cheeks. He used the long spoon to scoop some of the mound of whip cream and let it melt on his tongue.

"This is fabulous," he said. "They're doing a bunch of things right here. I haven't found anything better in New York."

"It is nice. They're guaranteed success."

"For sure," Kris said. "Look at the people lined up at the door. Good thing we came early."

"You said you have ideas for how we Christmas tree growers can dig our way out of problems," Marcie said. "I'd love to hear."

"I have several. Long-term, they involve how to consolidate marketing and shipping, almost a co-operative association in this area, but first we'd need a big event to boost our cause."

"Like what?"

"In New York City, my dinky office is high above Rockefeller Plaza. In the two years I've been there, one of the best benefits has been having a grandstand window view over the Plaza as the Christmas tree goes up."

"I'll bet." Her eyes shone. "I'd love to see that. Did you take pictures?"

"I don't have them with me, but I have a photo of the first Plaza tree if you want to see how the tradition began."

"Please."

He pulled a slim notebook from a jacket pocket. "They raised the first one Christmas Eve, 1931, during the Great Depression. That was a rough year, carloads of cut trees going to waste because nobody could afford to buy. The construction workers were happy to have jobs building the Rockefeller Center and spontaneously pooled their money to buy a twenty-foot balsam fir to put in the center area being cleared. They just decorated it with what their families made. Paper chains, cranberry string. Tin cans. Here's the picture."

He pulled printed sheets from the back pocket flap of his notebook. Marcie scooted her chair closer.

"Interesting. Very different from how it looks now."

"Yes, but that center area is still where they put up the tree. Two years later, the Rockefeller organization decided that erecting a huge, decorated tree would be their yearly tradition. A 'holiday beacon for New Yorkers and visitors.' That has happened." Kris grinned across the table. "And nowadays, they use Norway spruce exclusively for the Rockefeller tree."

"Uncle Halvor would love that." Marcie's dimples flashed.

Kris tapped the next printed sheet. "Here are the printed requirements from the Rockefeller committee. They say it has to be a Norway Spruce in the later years of its life cycle, measuring at least seventy-five feet tall and forty-five feet in diameter."

"That's massive."

"Yes, but you have some at the end of your driveway that big, I think. To enter, growers have to send a photo of the tree they want to be considered, with the grower standing next to it to show proportion."

"I can just see Uncle Halvor standing by one with a smile on his face."

"The only problem is so far they're not going beyond the three-state area around New York State. I'm working on them to consider the rest of us."

"Do many tree farmers apply?"

"Quite a few, from what I hear. After the season's over, workers remove the decorations and give the tree to a charity to mill for lumber for needed housing."

"That's another great idea."

"Which means more publicity because the tree grower gets credited again. Seriously, seeing the Rockefeller tree delivered and decorated twice from my bird's-eye window has gotten me thinking. While standing there watching the tree go up, I met one supervisor, Seamus O'Leary. I asked him to consider a Wisconsin entry since we're a huge Christmas tree-growing state. He said no for now. This year, for the first time, they're arranging a tree from Ottawa, Canada, to emphasize friendships between our nations, but he said he'll suggest Wisconsin and Midwestern states next time. I also have more ideas."

"I'll bet."

Their ice cream treats were melting. Marcie sipped more cherry phosphate, and Kris pushed his spoon deeper into the double chocolate malt, now too thick to pass through his straw. He turned to his next page of notes.

"You probably follow the yearly National Christmas Tree lightings in Washington D.C. Now they also organize special singing and other programs around it."

"I always try to watch on TV."

"We both love our Christmas trees." His eyes crinkled as he smiled at her, making Marcie's breath catch a little. She was glad when he continued without seeming to notice.

"Besides the National tree in Washington D.C., they also choose one each year for the White House that the First Lady decorates in a special theme. They select trees from across the U.S. to highlight our nation's size. They've chosen six from Wisconsin through the years. I think it's time for that to become seven."

She paused. "That's nice, but how does it benefit growers? If trees are donated, there's no pay."

"Think of the publicity. It's another televised event gaining national and international attention for growers and states."

"True."

Excitement entered Kris's voice. "Lady Bird Johnson does a fabulous job. She's already decided that this year, along with the usual ornaments, she's using fruits, nuts, popcorn, seedpods, gingerbread cookies, and wood roses from Hawaii."

"I can picture it." Marcie clasped her hands. "I love her national wildflower initiative. I'll bet she adds flower garlands of each state's flowers."

"Great idea!" Kris pulled out the next printed sheet. "So far, the National Tree outside can be any variety of evergreen. Some years, it's a cut tree. Others, they use a living tree with balled roots. Since 1954, the tree lighting ceremony also kicks off a three-week Pageant of Peace festival with nightly light, music, and art and religious observances."

"You've researched this well."

He nodded. "Because there's so much potential."

She was genuinely listening. Maybe there was potential with Marcie, too. Two years' age difference had seemed like a lot in high school, but now it was nothing. He was an idiot for not keeping in touch. At least she was with him today, smiling. Who knew where this could lead? He realized he had been holding her gaze a little longer than he meant to and tried to gather his scattered thoughts, shuffling the papers in his folder with a slight cough.

"They didn't string lights in the early years," he said, scrambling for something to say. "A General Electric engineer suggested that a bright national light display would encourage people to buy Christmas lights and use electricity."

"They were right," Marcie said. "There are fantastic light displays all over Madison. Even in Hudson, Christmas lights go on sale the day after Halloween."

"That's strategic marketing. New York City goes crazy with colorful light displays to keep the place as bright at night as it is during the day so it's *the city that never sleeps.*"

Marcie tapped her glass with a finger. "Is that good?"

"Frankly, it's too high geared for me. Someone convinced President Coolidge that if he personally lit the tree, it would increase the appeal of Christmas lights and the use of electricity. When he flipped the switch, twenty-five hundred red, green, and white electric bulbs flashed on."

"Can you imagine?"

"Barely. First Lady Coolidge was an amazing organizer. She had three thousand school kids sing while the U.S. Marine Band played carols and NBC radio broadcast it all."

Marcie leaned forward. "My mom said even before television days, her parents pulled chairs up to the radio to listen."

"My dad's parents did the same. I'm impressed that organizers gathered such huge crowds plus held the attention of a radio audience across America."

"And beyond. They obviously did many things right."

Once they finished their ice cream treats, their waitress stopped by.

"Can I get you two anything else?"

Marcie was a great sport for paying attention all this time. Kris looked at her and then to the shoppe's front. The waiting line now stretched from the front door half a block along the sidewalk.

"We've taken enough time, but it was delicious. We'll have to come back soon."

"Yes." Marcie blotted her mouth with her napkin. "I haven't had ice cream this good anywhere. Not even Madison, where they cater to university students."

The waitress slid a hand to her hip, smiling. "Our owner studied there and brought the idea back to his hometown."

"Great thinking," Kris said. "It's paying off. He saw a good idea and made it work."

They paid and stepped outside.

"There are plenty more facts and figures, Marcie, but I've already rattled off too many. I apologize for talking non-stop. I'm a numbers guy. Details fascinate me."

"I can see why you're so interested." She looked at her watch. "I'd better get home, though, before they think our rattletrap truck broke down again and send out a search party."

"Is that likely?" He looked her truck over. "I'd better follow you. Make sure you get home safely."

"I'll be fine, but it made strange sounds on the way here."

"That does it. Don't risk it." He smacked a fist into his other hand. "I'll follow you. Anyone raised on a farm learns mechanics along the way. I fixed my boss's new Porsche when it stalled near the Holland Tunnel."

"No kidding!" She raised her eyebrows. "That could have been bad."

"I didn't have the right tools, but jury-rigged it, and it worked. That impressed him so much, he took me home to meet his family. Told our office staff I'm his personal grease monkey and treats me better now."

She pulled her keys out of her purse. "Good men are

appreciated anywhere. Now, about Christmas trees—is there immediate action your dad or my uncle should take?"

"Not yet. I'm not telling Dad anything until I'm sure these options can work. In the next few days, I'll have more answers. There is some labor and expense involved."

Her keys rattled as she unlocked the door.

"Once I get more answers, are you willing to hear the rest?"

She gave him a charming smile. "Sure. When you have answers, give me a call."

His eyes widened. "Say, is your shipping shed just across the property line still there?"

"Yes. It's dilapidated and needs paint, but it's there."

"Remember the summer we left messages behind the eavestrough above the rain barrel? Is that plastic container still there?"

She flushed. "Last time I looked, it was."

He felt his face heat, too. "Why did we stop?"

Her eyes met his. "It just happened. You left for university."

"And didn't get home much. When I did, you were gone on 4-H trips or school competitions."

"We both stayed busy."

"You were County Fair princess and then went to State." His eyes stayed on hers. "You should have won."

"The Waukesha girl had more talent."

"That's not what I heard."

"You paid attention? That's ancient history." Marcie climbed inside the truck and rolled down the window. "I'm sure you've made many friends since. When it's the right time for friendships to grow, they do. If not, that's fine. Things work out the way they're meant to."

"Or sometimes they do later. We're still good friends, aren't we?"

"I guess." She brightened. "I've known you at least half my life."

"I'll look forward to next time."

"You might have to settle for a phone call. It was hard arranging to do my last semester here. I have to help Uncle Halvor all I can, plus finish research. The day you came home, you saw the horrible stress he's under. Ingrid, too. I want to decrease that."

"How's her health?"

"Balsam's residents talk too much." Marcie's lips tightened.

"They're concerned."

"It's her story, but if she takes care of herself and tries to avoid stress, she'll do better soon."

"I'd like to hear her story. I do wish them well."

"Beneath it all, I'm sure my uncle feels the same. Thanks for today."

"It bears repeating." He pointed back to the ice cream shoppe. "Let's do this again."

She started her engine. "If we can match schedules, every taste bud on my tongue says yes."

10

I t was amazing how excited Kris got while discussing Christmas tree selection possibilities. The chances of them being chosen seemed impossible, but he talked like they could. He was even more handsome when he got animated. No wonder he was successful in New York. How had he been there two years without some girl snapping him up? Probably someone there did have her cap set for him, whether he knew it or not. He was a great catch!

When Marcie picked up Saturday's mail, she saw another letter from the bank. Uncle Halvor grimaced when she handed it to him and slipped that envelope into his pocket, too.

He stayed quiet during dinner. After several minutes, Ingrid asked, "Halvor, are you feeling okay?"

"Fine," he muttered through tight lips.

Thankfully, Ingrid looked better, with more color in her cheeks. She didn't seem to tire as easily. Marcie and Halvor agreed to avoid discussing subjects that might upset her.

He sensed Ingrid watching him.

"Just too much work lately," he said. "Like it or not, I'm not as young as I used to be. I should take vitamins."

"That might be good," Ingrid said, "but I doubt that's your problem."

He sipped water. "Our Marcie's better help than any two hired men, but there's still plenty to do to get trees to market."

Ingrid frowned. "We have enough good trees to sell, don't we?"

"I think so." He touched her hand. "It's hard to be sure, but we'll manage somehow." He fidgeted with his fork, picking it up and laying it down without putting food on it.

"You're sure you're okay?" Ingrid repeated. "You're not eating, and you're thin to start with. I made Norwegian meatballs especially for you."

"Thank you. They're perfect—better than Swedish meatballs any day." He squeaked a laugh. "I'm not hungry when I'm this tired. I'll have some later." He laid his fork down. "I might not go to church in the morning. Sleeping in sounds good."

"What?" Ingrid looked at Marcie. "Have you ever heard him say that before?"

"Not even when they removed his gallbladder."

"He wouldn't stay in bed then. He overhauled engines on the kitchen table, so sometimes our food tasted like fuel, but I love him anyway." Ingrid covered his hand with hers. "Seriously, Halvor, you work too hard. How can we help? You wake up early each morning to tell the sun to rise."

"It's not that bad." He managed a smile. "We'll be fine."

The next day, he came to breakfast dressed in his coat and tie.

"I'm going to church after all. A man has his priorities."

"Good, dear. You remember we have two services now until New Year's. Which one do you want to go to?"

"I forgot. It sounds complicated."

"Not very, but I should tell Marcie. The traditional service is 9 a.m. and the contemporary at 10:30 a.m."

"I'll choose the traditional." He craned his neck and loosened his tie. "Which will the Lundquists attend?"

"Probably the contemporary." Ingrid drained her cup of very pale coffee.

"Good." Halvor rose. "Let's go."

They sat near the front since Ingrid would sing with the women's trio. During service announcements, Pastor Wallace Avery said, "Thank you, Karin Lundquist, for filling in with our women's trio on short notice. Ida Holmberg's grandbaby came early, so she rushed to her daughter's to help. Our trio will sing in both services to give everyone a treat."

The ladies sang in beautiful harmony and returned to their seats.

Halvor shifted to see where the Lundquists sat four rows back. Then he trained his eyes up front until Pastor Avery said, "Today's text is Proverbs 16:7. 'When a man's ways please the LORD, he makes even his enemies be at peace with him.'"

Halvor swallowed. Crimson climbed his neck. It rose above his starched white shirt collar to his ears and then up to the top of his head. He rested both hands on his knees, rocking slightly.

"Halvor?" Ingrid put a hand on his knee. When he didn't answer, she quietly repeated, "Halvor?" He jerked loose and rose to his feet. He windmilled his arms slowly as if fighting off assailants until one arm dropped.

Ingrid flamed crimson while trying to calm him. She tugged one arm. "Please sit down, dear."

He didn't seem to hear. His face twisted slightly askew.

Marcie reached over Ingrid to grasp her uncle. Something terrible had gripped him. The congregation watched as Ingrid stood and held Halvor's arms until he pulled free. When she placed a hand on the small of his back, he jerked and faced the pastor.

"Avery, don't preach out loud the things I tell you in private. It's not Christian. Who do you think you are? You put your pants on one leg at a time, just like me."

The pastor's mouth opened and closed twice, but no words came.

Halvor swung his arm as if the pastor's words were stinging bees to swat away.

Avery said. "Halvor, I didn't—"

"Don't deny it. I asked for wisdom, but things are too far gone." His voice rasped. "I'm telling you, telling you all, I won't give up, won't ask for help. I'll do it like my ancestors, by myself. And you bankers!" His eyes pinned several. "We served on committees together. Some friends you are!"

His lips buzzed with flecks of spit. "I shouldn't talk, my head aches so bad. Need fresh air."

His next sounds were garbled, but Halvor didn't notice. When Ingrid couldn't pull him back into his seat, Marcie stood.

"Uncle Halvor, let us help."

"Out!" He squeezed past them both, accidentally pushing Ingrid back into her seat. He reached the aisle and lunged for the front door.

Pastor Avery's wife, Wanda, dashed after him. As a nurse, she read the warning signs. Marcie raced along, too, but couldn't catch him.

When Halvor pushed open the oak front door, he staggered a moment as if struck. He stood unmoving like a mighty tree shuddering from the first ax blows that bring it down, hanging briefly motionless as time stopped. And then his left leg folded under him. He spun slightly and dropped heavily across the door's threshold.

"Dear Lord, help him," Pastor Avery exclaimed.

Wanda and Marcie closed in, but Kris reached Halvor first, bending to speak in his ear.

"Halvor, it's Kris. Can you hear me?"

His only response was mild tremors.

Kris motioned to Wanda. She nodded, and he stretched Halvor out more comfortably. Wanda checked his airway. She lifted his eyelids and, after finding his eyes rolled back, checked his wrist.

"His heart's steady."

"Thank God." Head bowed, Ingrid knelt at Halvor's side.

Marcie slipped an arm around Ingrid and rested a hand on her uncle's shoulder.

"Halvor?" Kris repeated. "Let us help. Squeeze my hand if you hear me."

Halvor's calloused hand lay still in Kris's strong one. He gave occasional soft moans and tremors.

Ingrid stroked his cheek. "Love, stay with us."

"Someone call for an ambulance," Pastor Wally instructed. "Sermon's over. Please all pray."

Several persons rushed to wall phones in the church. Lars Lundquist sprinted a block and a half to the volunteer fire station.

Watchers sighed with relief when they heard screaming sirens and saw flashing lights.

Marcie gripped Halvor's free hand while choking back tears. *Dear Lord, we need this good man. Please don't let us lose anyone else we love.*

And then, unable to hold back her grief, she yielded to quiet sobs.

Kris bent near. "Ingrid? Marcie? May I drive you to wherever they take him?"

"Bloomer or Eau Claire, I guess," Ingrid said. "I'll ride in the ambulance." She climbed into the back once the paramedics loaded him. "Marcie? We'll need our car. Will you follow, please?"

"Of course." Marcie still knelt next to Halvor.

"Are you okay?" Kris asked.

"No, but I will be. I have to be."

"Can I help?"

"Thanks. You have. I need to follow the ambulance."

Kris watched her go.

11

———

Through the long afternoon, while Dad assembled financial records, Kris updated notes on several New York City accounts and phoned them in. In between, he paced the family front porch, looking through the trees at the Halvorsen place, hoping to see activity.

Dad climbed the steps. "I doubt you'll see them home for a while. I'll be surprised if they get back tonight."

"Why don't we know anything? Pastor Avery and his wife haven't heard either. Someone should know something by now."

"I've phoned, too. The hospital won't give information to anyone who isn't family."

"Give me that number. I'll leave a message so Ingrid and Marcie know we're thinking of them."

"They know. Be patient. No news is good news."

"I hate it taking so long."

Dad hiked his eyebrows. "Did you forget things are slow in small hospitals on weekends? The ambulance took Halvor to Bloomer. That's good. If it were worse, they'd rush him to the Twin Cities or transport him by helicopter. He must be stable enough to keep overnight and do more tests tomorrow."

Kris shuddered. "It's rough. I wonder how Ingrid and Marcie

are holding up and if they have enough insurance." He crossed the porch again, squinting into the distance.

"Hard to say. I don't know their personal situation, except things have been tight."

"What do you think about his symptoms?"

Dad also stared toward the Halvorsen place. "I'm no medical man, but it looked like some kind of stroke or nervous exhaustion to me."

"That's what I think, too, but my university First Aid training practices seldom match what we see in real life."

"That's true. It's horrible seeing someone drop in front of you."

"He'll need help no matter how this turns out."

Dad gazed up as if the sky held answers. "What would that look like? We're all busy and strapped. I guess it depends on what ails him."

Kris paced more steps. "I hope what we saw is a mild stroke. Otherwise—"

"I know. It could knock him out for the season."

"Or longer. How are you coming with your financials? The sooner I start, the sooner I can finish."

"Sure." Dad's face reddened. "I need a little more time. You know I have trouble staying organized."

"Busy people do. Can I help?"

"Thanks, but it's a one-man job. Besides, I should teach myself a lesson. I'll have it first thing in the morning. Mom wants time with you tonight anyway."

"That sounds good."

When Kris walked into the living room, Mom was just ending a phone call. "This town is full of good-hearted people," she told him.

"What's up?"

"Whatever the Halvorsens are facing, that's the second phone call of people donating cash and wanting to form a work party to help."

Kris raised an eyebrow. "That's less likely to happen in big cities. Good, the Halvorsens can use it. What kind of work do you think they need done?"

"I imagine the same as any Christmas tree farm this time of year. Marcie will know. Prep to get things ready for sales. Repairs to their processing shed to prepare it for operation. I thought Marcie mentioned trimming off blight ends to market trees. I hope it works."

"I heard that, too. I looked at their shed. It's gone downhill. A coat of paint wouldn't hurt it either. And whatever else Marcie and Ingrid say will make things easier for Halvor—if he's able to come home soon." He opened his billfold and withdrew cash. "Put this with the other donations, Mom. And sign me up for a work party."

"Are you sure? That's a lot of money."

"I earned another bonus. But keep it anonymous." He moved to their front window. "Still no sign of life their way."

"I don't expect them home tonight. I will keep donations anonymous and share the word about a work party when I go to work tomorrow."

Kris turned. "When you go where tomorrow? What are you talking about?"

She flushed. "I guess I haven't told you. I hate to be gone with you home. It's only a few hours a day. I tried to switch shifts, but no one could trade."

He crossed his arms across his chest. "What's only a few hours? What are you doing?"

"The retirement home pays top rates when I cook the noon meal. Even outsiders come in to pay and eat. It's almost like we're a restaurant."

"I'll bet. They won't find anything better in town. If we weren't busy growing trees, you'd run a great restaurant."

"Except it ties people down so much. I just cook four meals a week—sometimes five. Ingrid was cooking breakfasts until she got sick. She wants to return to it."

"I don't like either of you needing to do that. You weren't doing that when I was home at Easter."

"No." She studied her fingernails. "Things get tight with taxes due. I'm glad to help. Cooking is easy for me, and the seniors are fun to be around. I doubt I'll do it forever."

"No, you won't. Just how bad is Dad's problem?"

"Let him tell you. He'll go through it tomorrow." She put a hand on Kris's arm. "Just remember, he's a good man who's hit hard times. Even good men make mistakes."

He could not read her eyes. "Now you have me worried."

"Just be prepared."

After releasing his arm, she sat on the couch and picked up their photo album.

"Sit here by me." She patted a place. "I'm going through family photos and ordering reprints for you in New York. Do you remember this?"

She pointed to a photo of him as a boy holding a cute small animal in his hands.

He slid closer. "Vaguely. How old was I? What animal is that?"

"You were six. It's a chinchilla. Do you remember when we had them?"

"Kind of. We had a few in cages. They were cute and cuddly. But then they were gone."

"They didn't work out. When your dad and I married, we started buying a small place near my folks in Chippewa Falls. Dad had a decent-paying maintenance job and heard about an investment that could move us ahead faster. The guy doing it was successful. Only, it didn't turn out for us like we'd been told."

"What was it?"

"Raising that cute little animal you're holding in the picture. What do you know about chinchillas?"

"I know they're used in making high-priced fur coats. I saw one coat in a Saks Fifth Avenue window that cost a fortune. My boss is buying his wife one."

"I'll bet. Chinchilla babies cost fifty dollars each. That's a significant investment. The breeder said they bred like rabbits. He was already raising them, so offered to board ours along with some he was taking care of for another investor. The literature said we could count on four kits per litter, but more often it averaged two, and then usually only one lived."

"I remember the one in that picture. I wanted it for a pet."

"They're adorable but high-strung. It was heartbreaking seeing one fine in the evening but dead by morning. When Dad would stop in, the breeder would pull out a dead kit he said was ours. It was always one excuse or another—the weather was too hot or too cold, a change in feed, an illness sweeping through the herd."

"Finally, we tried raising them at home but didn't do much better. They got diarrhea so easily." She wrinkled her nose. "By the time we smelled it starting, it was already too late. Years later, Dad ran into the other investor the breeder was caretaking for. He'd also been paying with kits and found his dying while the breeder's numbers increased."

"Sounds suspicious."

The space between Mom's eyebrows disappeared as her eyebrows met. "Dad's a good man who trusts easily. I did, too. We think we were duped. We had invested too much money and couldn't recover. The bank gave us an extra three-month grace period, but we couldn't catch up."

She passed a weary hand over her forehead. "I've blocked most of it from my memory on purpose."

She turned to the next page of photos.

"Here's our truck when we left piled high with belongings stacked every which way. We look like Oklahoma Dust Bowl survivors moving on."

She tried to laugh, but he heard the catch in her throat.

"That's why we moved?"

"Yes. The bank sold our place for what we had in it. We got nothing, so had to start over."

"But came here?"

"Not right away. We visited my cousin near Madison. He was growing Christmas trees and doing well. We soon found land was available at a better price up here."

"But how could you buy? Was your dad involved in that?"

"That's right. I hope you remember him." Mom pointed to the next photo.

Kris smiled. "He swung me high and made me whistles from green maple tree branches."

"Yes. He helped us get a fresh start without making us feel like failures. He knew your dad is a good man who got caught in one bad decision."

Kris raised his eyes. "One?"

She hesitated. "At that point, yes. Even smart people can get caught in get-rich-quick schemes."

"I've met a couple. So, Grandpa lent us the money, and we paid him back?"

"No. He signed a codicil in his will that gave me my inheritance early instead of when he passed away. That was our new start. We came just when Halvorsens had their auction. Here's a photo of the day we came here. You were seven. We were so excited."

He stood on the running board of a loaded truck next to Mom and Dad, all smiling broadly.

Kris leaned forward. "I still remember Dad saying, 'New days, new horizons,' as we came north. In some ways, your circumstances and having to sell out were similar to the Halvorsens'."

"I guess, but we were newcomers. We didn't know Halvor's situation, and he didn't know ours. We showed up at the auction and bought the land for a fair price. We loved having Dad work hard on our land for a living. It's mostly been good until now."

"This was a perfect place to grow up. Every kid should be so lucky."

"You ran and explored and convinced us we needed a dog."

Kris chuckled. "Lady was the best. Do you have early pictures of her?"

"Somewhere. I'll find some. Duke looks a lot like her."

"We had good years, but I also remember Dad several times buying equipment we couldn't afford that nearly sank us."

Mom sighed. "He has a hard time resisting good salesmen. I try to go with him most times but don't always manage."

"I thought things were fine when I was here at Easter. What happened?"

"That's been six months, Kris. A lot has happened since."

"Why didn't you call me?"

"Dad was embarrassed. He hoped to fix it and thought he could." She closed the photo album. "I still don't understand why he thought this investment would be a sure thing. It seemed guaranteed, and he wanted to surprise me. He met investors at a Chicago Chamber of Commerce Convention bankrolling a new Midwest television station. It would televise sports shows exclusively by subscription memberships. You know Midwesterners love their sports."

"Definitely."

"One man had connections to get an FCC operating license promising a high rate of return."

"Ah, the Federal Communications System," Kris said. "Their licensing can be tricky. The approval didn't happen?"

"Legislation passed making that kind of TV station ownership an illegal monopoly. Dad and the others challenged and ran up legal bills. It's over now. They couldn't keep going."

"How much did Dad lose?"

"I don't know. He had put a second mortgage on our place I didn't know about. Maybe I should handle our finances, but don't want him to feel belittled."

"I hear you. Sometimes it helps to have another person to be accountable to. So you're only cooking to help finances?"

"And to plug a few holes. I told Dad I loved being around older people, which is true." She twisted the Kleenex in her hands. "He's a kind, good man. We've been happy. He works hard, but his optimism gets the best of him."

"That's generous of you, Mom, but how much is the debt?"

"He'll show you in the morning." Her eyes lowered. "He wanted to help our family and didn't want you to think he had another problem."

"Could we lose this place?"

Mom hesitated. "Maybe. Everything depends on this season. We've been in the black most years. We're slipping now. It feels like déjà vu."

"I see," and Kris suddenly saw a great deal more than he wished.

She closed the album. "Do you mind if we quit discussing this? I'm getting a headache. Let's watch TV."

She checked her watch.

"Goodness, the Ed Sullivan show is starting, and tonight's line-up is fabulous. Frankie Valli and the Four Seasons, Connie Francis, Gwen Verdon, and Jimmy Durante!"

"That's super." Kris crossed the living room and turned on the set.

"Thanks. Durante makes me laugh." She glanced at Kris. "I'll bet we could both use a laugh tonight."

He moved close to where she sat on the couch and hugged her. "I love you, Mom."

Tears filled her eyes. "I love you back, son."

The comedian had Mom's attention in seconds. As she laughed and laughed again, the tension left her body. Durante closed with his trademark line, "What a revolting development this is!"

That sums up our place and the Halvorsens', Kris thought.

When the show ended, Mom and he both climbed the stairs to their bedrooms. Dad hadn't come in yet.

12

———

As soon as Pastor Avery knew the ambulance would take Halvor to Bloomer, he phoned a chaplain friend there, requesting help.

"Otis? There's a good man in our congregation knocked down by hard times. He's a Christmas tree grower. Lots of bills and pressures, blight problems. He collapsed in service today. No clear diagnosis yet, but they're bringing him to your hospital. Will you please check on him to make sure he gets the help he needs?"

"Sure. I owe you for a few times you've stood in for me."

"He's Halvor Halvorsen, a good Norwegian to the core. You're Scandinavian yourself, aren't you? Tell him."

"So, he only likes Norwegians? He thinks they're the only good people around."

"You hit that nail on the head. He needs a little educating."

"Okay. I've met others like that. Used to be a bit that way myself."

They chuckled.

"I don't know all his needs. Finances for sure, although I hope there could be some county or state funds. He'll need help

80

with farm chores for sure. People here already want to pull together work teams."

"That's big-hearted. Folks here are that way, too. Some of the finest people on earth."

"Exactly. I don't know how long he'll be laid up. It depends on his diagnosis and staying in Bloomer versus rehab somewhere else or coming home. His niece, Marcie, is with him and his wife, Ingrid. She's been ill recently as well. Precious people."

"I'll watch for them. It's no trouble. I enjoy interesting people."

Pastor Avery had to chuckle. "That's good, because Halvor qualifies."

MARCIE COULDN'T CATCH up with the ambulance, but she knew where it was going. After entering Bloomer Hospital's Patient Parking lot, she headed for the Emergency Room and found her aunt and uncle right away.

"The paramedics took good care of him all the way here," Ingrid said. "He calmed once they checked his vitals and administered oxygen. They gave him medication, too. I'll stay in the family waiting area tonight. They have recliners."

"What do they say it is?" Marcie asked quietly while a nurse did something with Halvor.

"They're guessing some kind of stroke. They judged him stable enough to stay here for the battery of tests when the neurologist comes tomorrow."

"That's great. Don't worry about me. I'll sleep in our car to save a motel bill."

"No, you won't. They offer family housing at a low cost. We're already set. I'll give you directions and a key."

13

All night, Kris kept thinking he heard a vehicle enter the Halvorsens' driveway but saw no fresh tire tracks in the morning. Just to make sure, he walked up the drive far enough to see the house and garage parking area. Nothing.

As he returned home, he found Dad sitting on the porch, putting on his boots.

"Getting an early start?" Kris asked.

"I thought I would. It's warm for early October." Dad mopped his face with a red bandana. "I'll check the moisture of the trees. If it stays this hot, I need to irrigate our trees again before frost."

"It's a good thing you got that water system installed."

"It is. Some things are expensive but end up being good insurance plans." He wiped his face again and tucked the bandana in his pocket.

Kris studied Dad. "You look pretty chipper after working late last night."

"I wanted to get everything ready." He glanced sideways at Kris. "Mom said you two had a good talk."

"Yes. She's an amazing woman. You're both terrific. But I

wish you'd felt free to tell me about the financial crunch sooner. Maybe I could have done something."

"I wanted to fix it. Thought I could." Dad finished lacing his boots and met Kris's eyes. "You know how it is. A fellow thinks that if he works hard enough, everything'll turn out right, but suddenly it's over."

Kris nodded. "I get that. We have one recent client that got burned that way."

"So, what do you say, son?" He clapped Kris's shoulder. "Let's eat enough breakfast to handle the job."

Kris nodded. "Mom's cooking should guarantee that. And then I'm ready to balance orders, sales, and accounts receivables to dig us out."

Dad didn't eat much.

As they crossed the porch, both men looked toward the Halvorsen place again.

"It's hard when neighbors are hurting," Lars said. "Halvorsen isn't always the nicest guy, but I hate seeing him in a bad way."

"I keep hoping we'll hear something or, better yet, see them drive in."

Dad paused. "I doubt it can happen that fast."

When they opened the front door, the aromas from Mom's cooking pulled them in.

Her warm smile embraced them. "Here are my two best guys. Sit and eat. Your lunch is in the fridge. I have to leave now but should be back by 3.30. Work hard. I hope everything untangles easily."

She kissed Lars's cheek and Kris's forehead before she breezed through the door.

Dad sighed. "I wish I had her energy. When it's time, I hope you find a bride like her."

"I'm in no hurry, but that's impossible. There's not another prize like her in the universe." Kris took seconds of hash browns.

They soon pushed back their chairs and carried their plates in the sink.

"Guess we should start," Lars said. "Let's work in the packing shed instead of hauling papers to the house. I keep most records out there."

"Fine."

They walked through tree rows to the boundary line dividing the two properties. The Lundquist packing shed stood on one side of the line, and Halvor's faded red shipping shed on the other.

"Both sheds were theirs," Dad said. "We adapted ours for our needs. Halvor's been spread so thin, his is getting run down."

"So I see."

Kris glanced at the Halvorsen shed. The rain barrel still stood under the eavestrough at its corner. It appeared that the small plastic container was still above it. That gave him an idea.

Dad entered their shed first, which looked like it always had. Ledgers lined up on the far counter by year. Clipboards itemizing receipts hung from nails along the wall.

"It's pretty straightforward," Dad said, "except more money's going out than coming in. We'll change that soon. This season's sales will take off and make the difference."

Kris paused. "I hope so. Is there any special reason you think so?"

"I'm an eternal optimist." Dad gave a feeble laugh. "Anyway, the paperwork's in order. Why don't I leave you here to look through it while I get irrigation going for the driest trees? I'll give you an hour? Hour and a half?"

"That should be fine. I remember how this part's organized, although I did more outdoor work in the past. If I have questions, I'll ask when you get back."

"Sure thing."

As Kris worked his way through the paperwork, things didn't add up. The dates and item numbers were clearly entered, but the supportive details didn't fit. Some paperwork must be missing. There had to be additional order and receipt records somewhere.

Dad was too far away for Kris to call to him. He'd look around to see what he could find. He opened cupboard doors and checked dusty shelves above the windows. Nothing.

Dad wouldn't throw important papers away. But bottom lines in the ledgers seemed to show their profits were in the black when according to Mom's concerns and Dad's troubled phone call, that wasn't true.

What's going on? Lord? Help!

Kris thought back to other seasons when he'd helped Dad reconcile records. It had been a while, but they'd done routine monthly audits and entered tax records. Dad's system should be the same now. Dad often walked the Christmas tree rows for stress relief or retreated to this shed. What kept him busy here so much? Kris recalled entering one afternoon when Dad hadn't expected him. In those first few seconds, it looked like Dad hastily hid something.

What was it? Where had he put it? Could Kris find it now? He scrutinized the shed space again and noticed a trapdoor cut into the floor directly under Dad's office chair. He didn't recall seeing it before. When Kris knelt and pressed one side of the square cover, one corner lifted, so he pulled it up.

The hole was filled with sawdust. He disturbed the top layer and encountered a battered metal fishing tackle box buried just below the surface. He'd seen that before. Why was it here now? Did it still hold the fishhooks, lures, floats, and bobbers they'd used when they'd gone fishing?

Kris smiled, remembering those good times when Dad taught him to tie feathered flies. They'd made great ones. Even won prizes twice at the county fair. Maybe when they got accounts straightened out, they could go fishing again.

He popped open the tackle box catches. It didn't hold fishing gear now. Instead, it held papers scribbled with IOUs and debt records, including a promissory note in Dad's name not listed in the ledger. Mom's name wasn't on it. There was also a book of unpaid overdue mortgage payment stubs. Instead of paying bills, it looked like Dad had invested too much in this last risky venture that he hoped would prosper when instead it might take the farm under.

But how could that be? How could everything change in six months? Could these be duplicate entries? Kris searched again, checking the stub numbers against the neat, itemized paperwork Dad had left on the counter to review.

These weren't duplicates. These were additional unpaid bills not posted or accounted for anywhere else. Could it be a mistake? Was Dad becoming just disorganized or delusional? Turning senile? Kris's heart hammered. Had he and Dad reversed roles? Dad looked strong and healthy, more than equal to a day's work, but these papers indicated a serious problem.

Kris's ears buzzed. His mouth went dry. Their family needed answers and cash soon, or they'd lose this place, too. He would approach Dad fairly—give him the benefit of the doubt. Maybe he'd forgotten how to post and reconcile entries. Or fallen hopelessly behind. Or been in a hurry. But why not say so and ask for help? There must be an explanation. If not, how could trust continue?

Through a window, he spotted Dad in the far rows, slowly heading his way. Kris wasn't ready to see him. If there were answers, he had no idea what they were. Their situation looked worse than Mom hinted, not better.

He needed time to think. A chance to cool down. He snapped the metal tackle box shut and grabbed its handle. He left the trap door partly open so Dad might see he'd found it. He raced to their house, needing to pray. To see if he could guess any explanation. But his stomach clenched with a horrible sinking sensation.

He needed to appreciate Dad, focus on his good points. Kris re-checked the dates on the mortgage stubs. They were badly in arrears. Maybe if Kris talked to the bankers in person ... He had big city know-how and knew banking jargon now. If he paid all late penalties, maybe they'd grant time to catch up on the standard back payments.

If Kris pulled his resources together, he could swing it. It would take all his savings and a bite out of investments, but that's what money was for, wasn't it? The bank would still make money, not lose, which kept bankers smiling. Guthrie had promised a raise at the end of this year. If Kris could keep his job and scrape by until then, a raise would help.

If his folks lost this place, Kris couldn't picture them being happy anywhere else. Especially not in New York City. He would always love and care for them the best he could, but he could not imagine a decent life for them in The Big Apple.

Mom was exceptional. She loved cooking. Maybe she could do that full-time here in Balsam. Dad was a gifted maintenance man. He could probably do that or janitorial work almost anywhere. The church had started building an annex offering subsidized housing for qualifying senior couples. There was talk of expanding the project later. Cramped living space, even with nice people, didn't sound ideal. But then another probability hit Kris.

What if the worst scenario happened to the Halvorsens, too? If it took Halvor time to gain strength, or he only recovered partially and lost their farm, they could need church housing, too. If things didn't change, they could be arch-rival neighbors in the same complex.

Kris rushed the rest of the way to the house before Dad saw him. At the porch, he thrust the metal tackle box into the opening behind the second step where he and his dog, Duke, used to hide years back when they didn't want to be found. It had worked then, and it would work now.

Kris had barely stepped inside the house when the phone shrilled. He caught it on the third ring. "Lundquist Farms."

"I'm glad to catch you, Kris." Mom's voice. "Have you and Dad talked yet?"

"We started but haven't had time to finish."

"Alright. I'm praying, but that's not why I called. Ingrid phoned Pastor Avery, and he reached me at work. We still don't know all their details, but she and Halvor will probably be gone a while. Pastor says donations are pouring in, and workers want to donate time but will need direction."

"That's true. If Marcie is busy helping Halvor or running things, maybe I could help direct volunteers."

"Good, son. Ingrid told Pastor that Marcie's driving home now to get clothing and other things they need. She should arrive soon. We prepared food for Marcie to take, plus piles of cards and messages I'll bring when I come home. Please catch her. Don't let her leave before I get there."

He looked out the window again toward the Halvorsen place. Still nothing. "I don't see Marcie yet, but I'll watch."

"I'm sure she'll come soon. Ingrid said she also had to pick up an order at the farm supply. Make her stay until I come."

"I will, Mom."

He had barely returned the phone receiver to its cradle when Marcie's car growled along the road like it had a bad muffler. She raced around the last curve before the blacktop descended to the river. Tires squealed into their driveway, raising dust plumes the whole way to the house before she braked hard and parked— the picture of a girl under pressure.

Kris wanted to see her. To help her. Inside the house, he splashed cold water on his face and combed his unruly hair. He didn't want her sensing his unease.

He sent up an emergency prayer. *Lord, give me strength to handle whatever comes to our family. And please help the Halvorsens, too.*

He grabbed his car keys and huffed out the air in his lungs to refill them with a deep, cleansing breath. This talk with Marcie needed to go well. So did his conversation with Dad, but right now, Marcie was his priority.

14

As Marcie ferried supplies from the car into the garage, she
heard a truck roar up their driveway. She stepped aside
from the rolls of twine and netting in the trunk to see who was
coming. Kris. In the farm truck. Fast.

She waited until he braked and killed the engine. "Is
everything all right?"

"Yes. I'm here asking how you are. And your uncle." His lean
form climbed out before the hot engine quit pinging.

"As good as can be expected. We don't know a lot yet." She
slid a hand to her hip. "How did you know I was home?"

"Mom phoned and asked me to find you. I saw you turn into
the driveway. Pastor Avery said cards and support are pouring in,
plus Mom and the retirement home staff have some things for
you. I'm not supposed to let you leave before she gets home at
3:30."

"Wow, there's a lot going on." She checked her watch. "I'll be
here that long but have to leave right after. I'm getting clothes
and toiletries they'll need in Bloomer. I'll go back and forth some
but mostly work here. I promised Ingrid I'd leave by 4:00 to be
there by dark, so I can't stay longer than that. She's got enough
to worry about."

89

"True. Do doctors know what Halvor's facing?"

"Because it's the weekend, they couldn't do much. They've ruled out a few things and are running more definitive tests. He's conscious and calmer. Still not the Uncle Halvor I know." She shook her head. "I hate seeing him like that. At least they're treating him close to home in Bloomer instead of the Twin Cities."

"That sounds like a good sign."

"Yes. His blood pressure was sky high when the ambulance got him. They're treating it like some degree of stroke. If that's what it is, we're praying for a decent recovery."

"I sure hope so." Kris nodded. "But I know even that can take a while."

He suddenly noticed more supplies in the back of her vehicle. "Here, I'll unload the rest." He lifted rolls of twine. "Where do you want these?"

"Against that garage wall for now. Thanks."

When they finished, Marcie closed the garage, and Kris dusted his hands.

"It's got to be hard with Ingrid not completely well yet, and now Halvor down."

"Yes, but I'm talking to the Lord about it. I'll give my best effort and see what happens."

"You've always been a plucky girl."

Marcie lowered her eyes under the warmth of his glance.

His voice deepened. "Your uncle is a proud man who likes things private, but any way you slice it, you'll need help. No person alone can do all the season prep and labor needed."

"I know." She looked away again. "I'll give my best effort but probably fail."

"There's no need to. About the work parties—I'm only here eleven more days, maybe less, but I'm a good organizer. If you name the biggest priorities, I can direct the men whether you're here or not. Actually, even if you don't have time to make a list, I pretty much know what needs doing on Christmas tree farms this time of year. Don't tell Halvor who's involved. Just say men from church. Or let him think it's Norwegian elves."

That brought a weary smile to her face.

"I know the routine. You can check and approve my list or add to it. What do you say?"

She managed another smile. "Do I have a choice?"

"No."

"That's what I thought. Then thanks. It means a lot. Why don't you step inside while I grab the other things we need?" She picked up items from the kitchen counter. "Here's a pen and paper if you want to start listing. I'm hoping he'll only be laid up a short time, but we don't know. Things don't always turn out the way we want. I know some jobs for sure that have to be done."

"So do I." Kris accepted the paper and pen. "Okay, I'm starting my list. When you have a minute, check it. I'll bet mine includes the things you'll put down."

"Probably." She collected items in the bathroom and stuck her head around the door. "That's very nice, Kris. Sit on the couch and make yourself comfortable. I can still hear you while I'm working. Thank you."

"You're welcome." He said nothing more until she looked his way again.

"Is something wrong?" she asked.

"Nope." He crossed a leg over one knee. "I'm just sorry things are so hard for you now. My timing stinks, but I don't know when there will be another chance to talk. I know more about the tree opportunities in Washington D.C. With Halvor sick, having a winning tree chosen could be even more important."

"I'm afraid it sounds like a pipe dream, but having a tree chosen could also help you, too."

"Frankly, we should both enter."

He changed position, shifting one leg over his other knee and then reversing the process.

"Marcie, I know I drowned you with a flood of words the

other day in Hudson. I'll cut it short now. The ice cream got me on a sugar high."

Her dimple flashed. "That could be it."

He pulled a printed list from his pocket.

"Here are the facts. US presidents have been lighting a National outdoor tree since 1929. President Coolidge lit his by touching a button while a searchlight from the Washington Monument also highlighted it. Two church choirs and the US Marine Band played carols until nearly midnight with nine thousand people present."

"Incredible." She entered the kitchen to grab a bag she added a few items to. "Wouldn't that be fabulous to see?"

"I hear the grower chosen often gets to go. A year later, Coolidge criticized cutting Christmas trees and announced he preferred to let them live."

"Ouch. That doesn't help growers."

"Nope, not at all. But Mrs. Coolidge decided to bring a living tree with balled roots inside to solve the problem. They found and planted a thirty-five-foot Norway spruce south of the Treasury Building and covered it with one thousand red, green, and white electric lights."

"What a huge effort. I didn't realize they made it such a big event."

"It got bigger yet." Kris leaned forward, tapping his pen against his notes. "When Theodore Roosevelt was in office, he banned Christmas trees inside the White House for 'environmental concerns' until one of his sons put up a tree in the White House kitchen. Roosevelt let it stay."

"I like that boy."

"So do I."

Marcie stacked clothes in a box she placed near the front door. "With all that's going on now, entering and having one of our trees considered seems like a dream. It could mean huge orders and support."

"Absolutely. And it's okay to dream." He put his notes back in his shirt pocket and waited for her to turn again.

"Marcie, I don't know your uncle's finances, but I think he's hurting. I'm still digging, trying to figure out my dad's situation. But I'd like them both to enter and have a tree chosen, whether it's for the National Christmas Tree or the one in the White House. Either would be a huge win for them and Wisconsin. We have a couple of big trees that I think could qualify. You have those two dandies at the end of your drive that are obvious prizewinners."

"Right. Grandpa Halvorsen planted those way back. They're balsam fir, while most of ours today are Norway spruce. Does the variety matter?"

"They choose different kids but mostly balsam and Norway spruce. It depends more on the tree's height, shape, and beauty. Basically, it boils down to the judge's choice."

"Great." Marcie laughed. "We should find that judge and bake him a cake."

"Except it's kept secret."

"I'm teasing," she smiled up at him and then sobered. "Would it matter if a little blight had been trimmed off?"

"I don't think so. Let's face it, growers have done that during bad years. When done carefully, no one can tell. If your uncle and my dad enter and we make it even to the top three, imagine the news coverage and boosted sales we'd have. I know Halvor's out of commission, and my dad and I have an issue right now, but if there were a way to show them the information ... let them think entering is their idea, not ours ..."

Marcie turned, hands on her hips.

"That's not a problem, Kris. My uncle's illness has changed things. Even with the best prognosis, he won't be back to full health for a while. Ingrid says all farm decisions are mine except for anything major I want to consult with them about. Frankly, I'd rather not bother them now. I'll do the preliminary entering and only tell them if we get high enough ratings to be seriously considered."

"Great!"

She stopped and looked around the room a moment for last things to take. "Imagine being finalists. The free publicity is any Christmas tree grower's dream."

"Exactly. They often truck in a gorgeous cut tree. Just picture it being yours or mine." Kris tapped his chin with his pen. "Just to be sure we're on the same page. Are you leaning toward entering the National Christmas Tree competition? Or for the White House tree the First Lady decorates?"

She grinned. "Why not apply for both? It can't hurt. Wouldn't that be splendid? Reaching the semi-finals in either would be life-changing."

"I agree. I'm glad you see the possibilities."

"Yes. This could work." Marcie's posture had straightened with her increased vivacity. "Halvor mentioned the chamber of commerce had a development fund that sometimes helped launch new projects. Do you think this could qualify?"

"I don't know. It's worth asking. There is some up-front expense. If chosen, we have to get our trees there. If one of us provides the National and the other the White House, maybe we could ship our trees together."

"It's great to have some answers. Along with using brainpower and elbow grease, we also need to pray for the Lord's help."

"Of course." Kris's face reddened. "I am praying for your uncle and aunt and you. I feel bad about the fix they're in. But the National and White House Tree Committees won't hear of us if we don't walk up to the White House front door and knock."

"I like the way that sounds." Her dimple flashed again.

"That's one thing working in New York has done for me. Made me a go-getter."

"I see that." Marcie put the last few items in her aunt's

carrying bag and closed its top. "Lead the way and tell me what to do, Kris. I'm on board."

"I have printed copies of the requirements. I'll give you one when you come to our house to get the stuff."

"Super. I'm ready."

He carried the box of clothes to her car and returned to help with smaller bags. As they turned to leave, her phone rang, and she answered.

"Hello? Yes, Kris Lundquist is here. Who's calling?" she paused, her face changing expression as she listened. Her eyes darted to Kris.

"It's for you," she whispered. "Morgan Guthrie, your boss."

He walked to the phone.

"Hello, sir. Yes, I'm at a neighbor's. No, I haven't solved Dad's problem yet, but we're making progress."

He chuckled.

"You think I'm a miracle worker if you want me to wrap it up in a week. Thanks for your confidence, but we agreed on two weeks." He paused to listen.

"I see. When did the merger happen? I know things happen fast in New York, but I don't see how I can return that fast."

He held the phone away from his ear.

"How much bonus? That's generous. I can't promise, but I'll review my work here carefully and get back to you. Yes, I phoned your secretary three times with updates. I'm glad they helped. Laura says what?"

He reddened.

"Tell her hi, too. Well, today is Monday. Let's say I get back to you Thursday night." He shook his head. "All right, Wednesday noon. Thanks. The same to you, sir. Goodbye."

Kris hung up the phone and stared at the wall. "How did he find me?"

"I don't know," Marcie said. "Probably your folks gave this number, but it's pretty clear what he wanted. He sounds like a man who usually gets what he wants."

"You're right. It's nice to be appreciated, but my boss doesn't own me. He approved me using vacation time to be here for two weeks. Helping Dad and your uncle will take every bit of that."

She rested a hand on his arm. "Kris. It's fine. You don't owe us anything. Just do what's good for you.

"But I want to help." His forehead furrowed. "I don't feel my time here is done. There's so much I can do to make things go better. For my folks. And your situation." He sighed. "I need to do some serious thinking."

"Yes, you do. I'll pray for you." She picked up her keys and purse. "Now, if your mom is home, I'll pick up what she has and head to Bloomer."

She stepped back to let Kris leave the house ahead of her. And then she locked the door behind them.

15

Kris was relieved to see Mom's car at the house. As soon as he and Marcie reached the porch, Mom opened the door and wrapped Marcie in a hug.

"So good to see you. I'm sorry, dear, for all you're all going through. How is Halvor? How is Ingrid?"

Marcie hugged her back. "She's better now that he seems more stable. He's making sense, he just can't control that one arm or leg much. We should know more soon."

"That sounds fairly good. I know you have to rush back, but Pastor wants you to have these cards and messages. He says most cards have donations inside with more promised. Phone calls are pouring in, but the mail takes a while." She handed Marcie a big handful of assorted envelopes.

Marcie sighed. "That's touching when so many people are having hard times themselves."

"That's what small towns do. We know how to pull together and look after our own."

Ingrid turned and pointed to a large ice chest.

"Our retirement home staff fixed things for you to have there for convenience and to save money. I'm sure the hospital needs to monitor what Halvor eats, but this should help you. I packed it in our portable ice chest. Keep it as long as you need it; we're not going anywhere during tree season."

Marcie opened its lid to see food packaged in bags and more in neatly stacked labeled Tupperware containers.

"I don't know what to say. You've done so much, and I don't even know who all was involved. For sure this will last all week."

"That's the idea, and there'll be more when you need it. It's properly cooked and refrigerated, so should keep just fine."

Marcie was bending to lift it when Kris said, "Leave it. I'll put it in your car."

"Thanks."

Dad walked in and also hugged Marcie. "What's the news, do they know more? How's Halvor looking?"

"Better than when you saw him, but very frustrated by his limitations. It's probably some kind of stroke. They'll know more when additional test results come in."

Dad looked at Kris. "Did Guthrie reach you? He called here first. I hope it was okay to give him your number, Marcie."

"Sure, that was fine."

"He also said his daughter wanted to talk to you, Kris."

"Yeah. He reached me. I'll take care of it." *Dad, quit talking.*

Dad looked relaxed. Congenial. He must have been inside the shed by now and seen the trap door open but wasn't saying anything. Fine, because Kris wasn't ready to talk, either. He turned. "I'll be right back. I have to go to my room for something."

He returned and gave Marcie the pamphlet with US Capitol Christmas Tree details without letting his parents see what he handed her. "Read this when you get a chance. Let me know what you think."

"I will." She put it in her purse without looking at it.

She turned to his folks. "Thanks again. I appreciate everything but have to leave now so Aunt Ingrid won't worry."

"Yes, she has enough on her plate," Mom said. "If Halvor

seems open, please give him our love. Tell them both we're praying for improvement."

Mom hugged Marcie again.

Kris walked her to the car and found room to tuck the cooler in the back seat.

"Drive safe," he said. "I'm serious about coordinating work parties. I'll bet my job list will nearly match yours."

"We'll see. I should be back sometime tomorrow."

He watched her drive out of sight. He was watching her drive away too often. Why was he the only one in his family who didn't hug her? Because her uncle would lynch him when he got well? Nope. That thought didn't intimidate him much, but life was complicated.

He trudged toward the house and found Dad waiting on the porch.

"Can we talk out here, Kris?"

"Sure."

They sat on the top step facing each other.

Dad didn't look relaxed now. His face had screwed up tight like a shrunken apple. His breath came in shaky gasps. *Dear Lord, don't let Dad get sick.*

"You found my box. I hoped you would. Smart boy."

"But what does it all mean? What happened?"

"I don't even know." He lowered his head into his hands. His shoulders shook. "I work hard for an honest living. We've made gains. You know we had some good years. When things started going downhill, I hopped onto an investment scheme without researching it enough. Trusted too much with funds we really couldn't afford to spare. When cracks started blowing the thing apart, it was like the Titanic hitting an iceberg and going down."

Dad looked up through red, watery eyes.

"Can you do anything to save our place? Any New York tricks? Maybe transfer the title and assets to Mom so she's secure and we don't lose everything?"

"Do you have a list somewhere totaling the true debts and assets?"

Dad nodded. "It's got lines through them and other numbers written in, but the basics are there. I mean, it got to where my brain scrambles when I look at it. Can't make sense of it at all. Kept hoping if I waited another day, it would start making sense again. I'm so sorry!"

"I believe you. I need to see your list."

"Yeah. I should have manned up and given it to you months ago, but I'm ready for you to take charge now. I'll do whatever you say."

Better late than never. Kris slid closer on the step. "I can't say I fully understand, but you're my dad, and I love you. I'm not here to judge you. We'll pick up the pieces the best we can."

Those words made Dad drop his head again. "Th-thanks, son."

"I have to be honest in saying I'm not completely sure what can be done. It might be too late, but I'm fairly creative. We'll have to repost every true number, nothing missing."

"We will."

"My New York savings should almost cover back mortgage payments and penalties. That's where we have to start. Do you want to come with me? Or do you want to sign a power of attorney to make me your representative?"

Dad's voice was a whisper. "For now, through the worst of it, I'd like you to handle it. I can't hold my head up in front of them."

"That's fine. Those arrangements are often temporary. If we write it out tonight, I'll go to the bank first thing tomorrow and talk face to face."

Dad's voice dropped lower. "Thanks. I wasn't sure anything could be done. I hoped you'd help. And, son?"

"Yes?"

"Mom doesn't know everything. Please don't tell her how bad it is. I hope she'll still love me."

He wept.

Kris sighed. "She has a pretty clear picture, and she does love you. You're a blessed man."

Dad's shoulders shook. "I don't deserve her. We need a miracle."

"You're right. We'll pray for one."

Anger melted as Kris put his arms around his dad's broad shoulders and pulled him close.

"I've developed some financial skills in New York. I can't guarantee how successful I'll be, but I'll do my best tomorrow. With fingers crossed and prayers said, there's a chance we'll survive."

16

When Marcie reached Bloomer Hospital, she searched for Halvor and Ingrid before unloading the car. She found them in intensive care. She walked in just as the primary doctor on call also arrived.

"Mr. and Mrs. Halvorsen?" He snapped open a metal clipboard to review the paperwork. "I added another round to my day to give you feedback."

"Thank you." Ingrid breathed a sigh of relief. "We're grateful."

"Of course. We have today's first imaging study back. We take cerebrospinal fluid from around the brain and replace it with air. That makes the brain's density show up in contrast on x-rays. The first picture inside your head shows quite a bit, Mr. Halvorsen. You probably had a series of mini-strokes over time without realizing it. There is clear evidence of stroke now."

Halvor spoke slowly, struggling to get his words out. "Shpected that."

"Blood tests rule out diabetes, so your slightly slurred speech isn't from that. You've experienced some facial paralysis, confusion, and muscle weakness, especially on your left side. We're doing further bloodwork and another series of tests.

Together those results will pinpoint your physical and speech effects and help us make an effective recovery and therapy plan."

"Wazh a stroke?" Halvor asked, working to enunciate. "My dad had younger me. Sawt coming. He couldn't lego."

"Things often happen in family patterns."

Halvor shuddered. "Died young. Fell like a cut tree." His eyes welled, and Ingrid gently took over his line of questioning.

"How bad is it? Can you help him? Please tell us in simple terms," Ingrid urged.

"I'll try. I'm glad to say we can do more these days than in your father's time. Again, all your information isn't back, but so far, you're a fortunate man. Your first good luck was getting medical help right away. The results could have been very different if you'd collapsed working alone on your farm or something like that. We're taking every step to get a clear diagnosis, but I'd say you have a good chance for a reasonable recovery. With hard work, you should regain most of your previous level of health. Also, a clot-busting balloon catheter was invented a few years ago. You reached us fast enough to receive that procedure, and it often makes a world of difference.

"Fabulous," Ingrid said.

"Only fair? Why izz that?" As Halvor's face flushed, his words slurred a little more.

"Uncle Halvor, it's okay," Marcie interrupted. "Doctor, I'm their niece. Break it down simply so we can do everything possible to help him."

After glancing at the clock on the wall, the doctor sighed, pulled up a chair, and sat.

"It's been a long day, but I want to help. Keep asking questions until you get what you need from me. In simplest terms, it's like lint gets caught in the brain cells and clogs communication. The human body has phenomenal repair abilities of its own. Modern medicine makes a huge difference when received in time, which your uncle was. But many of our efforts are helping support the body in what it does best."

The doctor studied Halvor. "Of course, the patient's cooperation with exercise and therapy protocols is an essential part of the equation. Plus, there are mental health guidelines for helping patients adjust to day-to-day stress from physical restrictions."

"Balderdash." Halvor hunched his hospital gown-clad shoulders together and squinted. "Thazz medical gobbledygook."

"Excuse me?" The doctor's mouth hung open.

"How can I work? Can't juzz lay around—" he stumbled. "Can't juzz leave it to—" he stumbled again, one hand fluttering in frustration before finally sweeping toward his wife and niece.

"Of course not. Full recovery is your goal. If further tests confirm our findings, you'll be in the hospital here at least this week. Next, we may find an opening for you in a nearby rehab treatment center while you learn exercise regimes and therapies somewhere closer to your home. We hope to put you on a road to recovery that brings you back to maximum strength and mobility."

"Sooner, not later, doctor. Need to be one deciding fudjure."

"Understood. But you need help considering options. Depending on how well you do, once you regain strength, you may advance to outpatient rehab appointments or have someone come to your home to work with you there if you agree."

Halvor worked hard not to slur. "Of courze. Whatever helps in shortest time."

Ingrid covered Halvor's hand with hers. "Do you see a timeline, doctor?" she asked.

"Not yet, but some thoughts are forming." He closed his clipboard and waited for Halvor's eyes to meet his. "If all goes well and you cooperate, you may be home in three or four weeks. On the other hand, it could take three or four months. The timing depends on the individual. I'll know more as your pattern becomes clear."

Halvor clenched his good fist as his blue eyes misted. "It can't take long, doc. Not half that!"

The doctor sighed. "Please understand you're already a very fortunate man. This is not a time in your life to push yourself. This easily could have led to an irreversible condition or even death. You're on shaky ground. If you cooperate, you'll improve. If you push unwisely and don't cooperate, your outcome will be worse. It's your choice."

He quit speaking until Halvor turned to face him.

"Your job is to cooperate and rest. If you're a praying man, I recommend that. Your outcome largely rests in God's hands. Make smart choices. And have a good night. I'll see you again tomorrow."

Ingrid squeezed Halvor's good hand. "Please listen."

Halvor didn't answer.

The doctor had just left when an apple-cheeked, gray-haired man whooshed through the side door.

"Are you Halvor Halvorsen and family?"

"Yes," Ingrid answered. "I'm his wife. This is our niece, Marcie."

"Pleased to meet you." He shook both women's hands and stepped near the bed to lightly grasp Halvor's shoulder.

"I'm Otis Swanson, one of two chaplains here. My friend, Pastor Wally Avery, just phoned from Balsam. He'll come in a few days if you're still here but asked me to see you now."

He dropped his elbows and hooked his thumbs onto his belt.

"Are they treating you right? Do you need anything?"

Halvor's rigid lips relaxed, "No complainsh."

"I hear you grow trees," Swanson continued. "I'm a retired farmer myself. We have that in common. It's hard being flat on your back when there's farm work back home."

"Ya."

"There's never a good time for a farmer to be away, is there?"

"Nope." Halvor turned to see the chaplain better. "How come you retired?"

"It was hard. A health scare put me on this path. I still farm some, have dirt beneath my nails."

As the chaplain extended a hand, Halvor offered his. Both had blunt nails with dark smudges under their nail ends.

"Good. We understand each other," the chaplain said. "With a name like Halvorsen, I figure you're a good Scandinavian like me."

"Nope." Halvor shook his head. "Pure Norwegian." He licked his dry lips until Ingrid helped him sip water. "Three generations, straight off the boat. Homesteaders, proud of 'em."

Swanson tapped his chest. "I'm a Swede, which I'm sure you'll agree is the next best thing to Norwegian."

Halvor fidgeted. "Nope, don't agree. N for Norway comes before S for Sweden in my alphabet."

Swanson chuckled. "In my alphabet, D for Denmark and F for Finland come before either of those. They fought wars among themselves, proving nothing, just damaging their countries from pride in the wrong things."

Halvor arched an eyebrow. "You mean they shoulda fought a common enemy instead?"

"Yup. They would have been better off and stronger today."

Marcie beamed to see her uncle warm to this chaplain who also loved the land.

A cheerful floor nurse walked in.

"We need more bloodwork, Mr. Halvorsen."

"Suckin' me drier than moshquitoes."

She giggled as if he had told a clever joke, and he smiled.

"If your guests will step aside, I'll draw the bed curtain for your vitals and a blood draw."

"I'll be going." Swanson grasped Halvor's shoulder lightly again. "I'll keep you in my prayers and see you tomorrow with reading material if you can manage it."

"Dunno. Maybe."

When the nurse finished and opened the curtain, Marcie handed her aunt and uncle the cards, donations, and gifts people had sent.

"You won't believe it," she said, face glowing. "They also sent a cooler filled with great food to last us a week if we need it."

Ingrid smiled. "There's no people like Balsam people."

"Who?" Halvor barked.

"Church ladies and retirement home staff. Why?"

"Names?"

"I didn't see names. Just caring church people and retirement center employees wanting to help. Does it matter?"

"Maybe." His eyebrows bristled. "How can we thank people if we don't know? I know some people didn't."

Marcie pulled over a chair and sat by her aunt. "Actually, everyone there wishes you well. If you think it's a problem to thank them without knowing names, write a letter thanking the whole church and the retirement home workers, so they're all included. But what they really want is for you to get well."

He stared from beneath shaggy brows.

"Hmmph. Being sick is embarrassing. How much of a fool did I look, Ingrid? Look stupid? Remember an awful headache and rush outside. Heard an ambulance siren, nothing else until here."

Ingrid took his good hand again. "You acted no different than any man your age with a health crisis. We've done hospital visits and seen sick people. You know what it's like."

"Embarrassing," he said.

"Not bad. Just not yourself. Now it's time to get better."

"Can't be sick. Too much to do," he almost wailed. He thrashed against his pillow, trying to push himself up, but fell back.

"Halvor. Be still and lie down." Ingrid's voice held an authority Marcie had not heard before.

He sank against the pillow but fussed, "No time, I have to get home. Marcie can't do all."

"Uncle Halvor, some Balsam neighbors want to organize work parties to help with things that need doing before our sales season starts."

He stiffened. "What? Other men on our place?"

"Is that so bad? You've done it for others. It's probably women, too, and teenagers—all kinds of people. We need help, and God is sending it."

"A man hash pride."

"Maybe too much. Look where it got you." Ingrid pointed to the hospital bed.

He gestured for water. Ingrid held the glass and straw to his lips.

"If people come work," he said after a minute, "don't tell me who. I can't stand being beholden." He dabbed his eyes.

Marcie stepped closer.

"Listen. What if it were Ingrid or me? You'd want us to behave and get well. What if resting and doing what doctors say gets you on your feet and stronger sooner? What then? You'd say we were fools if we needed that and didn't listen."

"Maybe." He slanted an eye. "Meddling?"

She returned a steady gaze. "No. Just telling the truth."

"You need to think straight." Ingrid stroked his cheek.

He drew several breaths. "Thank the helpers. Ingrid? Write letters? Find right wordz so soundz nice?"

She kissed his cheek. "I'll try."

"But I don't want you worn out," he fumed.

"Doing right things makes me stronger, not weaker," she said.

Marcie bent and kissed his other cheek. "Uncle Halvor, I know you're a sweetheart, but it's good to let other people see it, too."

He humphed again, tugging at his gown's neck, and turned a healthier pink.

"Why are folks kind? I'm a cranky coot. Don't deserve it."

"Halvor, stop. Who measures such things?" Ingrid said. "Ask the chaplain next time he's here. Maybe he'll teach you more about the goodness of God."

"Rather hear farming stories." But his lips twitched.

"Listen to both." Marcie stood. I'm happy you're some

better. We're praying for a full recovery. You know how much work needs doing on the farm, so understand if I can't come every day. You remember the challenges we discussed."

His eyelids fluttered. "I do. Can't forget."

"It's almost harvest time. The weather may change—"

He exhaled loudly. "Take charge, Marcie. Trust you."

"Good. I'll stay tonight to hear your test results in the morning and then drive home and work like crazy. When they transfer you from here to rehab or whatever happens next, phone me. I'll bring the car for you. Sound fair?"

"Ya," Halvor said.

"Good. I'll take the cooler to the place where we'll stay. Do you want to see some of the treats inside?"

"Maybe." Halvor shifted and craned his neck.

She lifted the cooler's lid to reveal an amazing array of foods —and the name Lundquist stenciled across the underside.

"Aarrghhh," Halvor slumped flat onto the bed.

17

From his years in Balsam helping Dad with accounts and records, Kris knew most of the bank's officers and staff. Lundquist Farms had paid its yearly loans on time with one exception, which quickly got made right. When he had been here last Easter and taken tax records to the bank, everything seemed fine. A teller had brought him hot coffee without his asking. The new loan officer he'd gone to school with asked if he had learned to play the rich man's game of golf yet to get ahead in New York.

"Not yet. Probably someday." Kris grinned. "So far, some of my best new clients are people I meet at the gym."

They shared a laugh.

Kris had interacted with these local people for years—planning Fourth of July and other holiday picnics and parades, serving on town decorating committees, especially at Christmas. He and Dad had made cash and tree donations besides contributing hard work.

Today after arriving at 9:05 a.m., Kris suddenly felt like a leper. The bank president looked up from his desk as Kris entered but quickly looked down again. The same loan officer he'd laughed with about golf at Easter ignored him now.

"Hi, James," Kris said, starting to extend his hand for a shake.

"Hi, Kris," James said but kept walking.

Kris stood still, recovering his confidence, when Lisa Scholz spotted him. She juggled the tray of coffee and small cookies prepared for the president's desk and walked over to shake his hand.

"It's nice to see you. Dave said you were in town. We hope you'll come by."

Kris beamed at this friend who'd just brightened his day. "That might work out."

"What can I help you with today?" She gave a genuine smile.

"A few minutes with your boss, but I don't have an appointment. It will only take him a moment to review this paperwork. Then I'll write him a check."

He opened the manila folder holding two pages of numbers, unpaid mortgage stubs, and his checkbook.

"Sure, Kris. I'll see if he's free."

She carried the tray of coffee and cookies into the president's office and placed it on the solid walnut credenza behind his desk. She bent her head and spoke pleasantly. His body language spoke volumes. He looked at his watch, and past Lisa at Kris, and then tapped a finger against his desk calendar before staring at Lisa again. Without smiling.

Kris had to hand it to her. After Lisa spoke to the president another time, he sighed and renewed eye contact with Kris. Then he stood and waved him in as if this were the first time he'd seen him today.

"Kris. How's the big city treating you?" he boomed in a warm voice when Kris walked in, grasping his hand and pumping it up and down like a farm pump handle. "I hear great things about you, great things—hometown hero makes good! Didn't I see a write-up in the *Balsam Times*?"

"Don't trust everything you hear. Make sure my folks didn't write it. They're my fan club."

"Haha, I know how parents are."

"Things are going well." Kris shifted from one foot to the other. "I'm learning the business and earning bonuses."

"That's great. Do you have time to sit? Or are you in a hurry?"

"I'll sit briefly but don't need much time. I know you're a very busy man."

"Yes, business is demanding, even in Balsam."

Kris sat.

"Going over things with Dad, I've found a problem we need to fix. He's a great guy but not good on details. He's missed a few payments and been overwhelmed lately."

"Many clients have. Hard times."

"He couldn't come in today, but I have his power of attorney. I'm here to solve the problem." Kris opened his folder and removed the mortgage-due stubs and his checkbook.

The president's eyes focused on the checkbook.

"Doublecheck me on late payment penalties. I'm paying everything in full today to catch up."

"Excellent." The president's eyebrows rose. "It's a sizable sum. Either your farm is making more money than I thought, or you're doing well in New York."

"Both. Dad always taught me that hard work pays off. He's a great role model."

"I'm sure he is, although he's had some trouble lately. I thought you might be coming in requesting a loan."

"No. That's not necessary. And we expect great sales this season."

"Really." His eyebrows rose still higher. "That is good news." He waved a hand. "Look, I'd forgive your late payment penalties if I could, but I'm limited by bank policy. I hear your employer, Guthrie, is a shrewd cutthroat himself."

Kris considered that statement.

"He holds out for good deals, but no more than other successful New York businessmen. He's shrewd but fair. After all, we are businessmen, not operating a charity."

The president boomed a laugh. "Good point. I have some personal clout. Let me cut your late charges in half."

Kris waved a hand. "No need. It was an oversight on our part."

"I insist. Let's see what that reduces your amount to."

The banker leaned over his calculator and deftly entered numbers, making his fingers fly and the machine sing. When its whirring stopped, he wrote a final number on the paper and handed it to Kris.

"Here you are. Significant savings, and that's the least I can do for a good friend."

"Thanks. Very appreciated." Kris wrote and signed a check, tore it out of his checkbook, and handed it over.

The banker palmed it. "Thanks, Kris. Remember when you're ready to expand or need new equipment, we want your business."

"Always." Kris chuckled. "Besides, you're the only bank in town."

They shook hands again.

Kris thanked Lisa on his way out the door and from there headed to Balsam's Best Hardware store down the street.

"Nice to see you, Kris. What can I do for you?" the proprietor asked after exchanging greetings.

"I need two standard hose clamps and another pair of your best hand pruners. Dad and I have lots of trimming to do."

"I'll bet. It's getting to be that season. This is my best brand, great ratings."

The proprietor laid the pruners on the counter next to the cash register. "Anything else?"

Kris stared through the window a moment but, instead of seeing Main Street, saw a scene near home.

"As a matter of fact, I do need something else. I'll drive my truck closer to load it. I need to do some brightening up. Give me three gallons of your best red-barn exterior paint and rent me a sprayer for twenty-four hours."

"Sure thing. You doing a fixer-upper project?"

"Something like that. I'll get my truck while you ring up my bill."

18

It took Marcie longer to return to Balsam than she expected. Her head whirled with tasks to be done, swarming like mosquitoes. Stop at the bank to establish the power-of-attorney note. Arrange a wheelchair ramp. Could he ever drive equipment again? He had to get well. Anything else was unthinkable. His head masterminded farm details.

How could she do everything needed in time for Christmas sales? Thank God church folks wanted to help, but she couldn't take time to give them direction. Had Kris been serious when he offered to do that? His boss wanted him back in New York. Seemed the boss's daughter did, too.

Lord, I'm overwhelmed. Nearly swallowed whole. Everything depends on this season. Keep my head screwed on straight to make good decisions.

As she entered their driveway, the setting October sun glowed like a crimson ball where it touched the horizon. She peered through the windshield. Wait! Was something actually on fire? As she entered the driveway, she braked hard to stop and get a better look. It appeared that the shipping shed was burning, but she didn't see or smell smoke. The entire shed seemed bright with flames. She drove closer, parked, and ran.

She saw a Lundquist truck parked on their dirt access road. What was Kris or his dad doing here?

Just then, Kris loped across the open grassy space between trees carrying several gallon paint cans and giving her an easy smile. His pick-up's flatbed held a metal apparatus that looked like a paint sprayer.

"You caught me." Kris grinned as she closed the space between them.

"What are you doing?"

"Isn't it obvious?" He waved toward the shed. "Looks better, don't you think?"

"But what have you done and why?" Her hands flared to her hips.

"It needed painting. I did it."

"You sure did." She expelled her breath in a huff. "It's nice, and of course we'll pay you, but money is tight."

His smile fled. "Marcie, no one's asking you to pay. It's a gift, my volunteer service to help. Are you saying you don't like it?"

"Oh, Kris, I do, but ..." She reached up and pushed her hair back behind both ears as if she'd run a track event and needed to cool down. "Bright red is how it should look, like it did when I first came, but Halvor has such a hard time accepting help."

"He doesn't have to know who did it." Kris stood still, holding a gallon paint can in each hand. "What about you, Marcie? Can you accept help? Because there are folks lined up who want to give it."

"That's amazing, and we need it, but it's hard. Halvor will ask who did each job so he can pay them back. I'm not sure what caused his condition, but I don't want to set him off again."

Kris placed the rattling cans in the truck bed and faced her. "Are you saying I should have asked you first?"

"Not exactly." Her shoulders sagged. "We can only pay for essentials right now, not cosmetic jobs."

She raised her hands to her head. "I mean, it looks great. It's nice of you to do this when you have work at your place. But what if having people work here makes Halvor worse?"

"That seems strange. Don't you mean having Lundquists involved could make him worse?"

"Partly." She jammed her hands into her pockets. "Kris. I'm sorry. This whole situation is a mess. You've done a wonderful thing, but I walk on eggshells with him. I don't want to see him worse."

"I read you. And this feud is a mess." He hiked his shoulders. "I guess I shouldn't have done this without checking, but I meant it for a nice surprise."

"I know." Her lower lip trembled. Next, tears would come. She would *not* cry. "Thanks for your time and effort. I have to go slowly and think things through. My uncle's been so good to me. I don't want to push him past his limits."

"I hear you." His foot flattened a dirt pile. "But he can't give direction right now. Finish your list. I have mine. Men from church want to help, and you need things done. When you're ready, let me know. If I'm still here, I'll supervise."

"You might not be here?"

But he just tipped his fingers in a salute, swung into his truck, and drove off in a cloud of dust.

Her eyes followed and stopped on the two giant sentinel trees marking the start of the driveway. Both would be prizewinners in any national contest. But if cut down, the whole world would notice their absence.

19

Relieved at how well things had worked out at the bank, Dad was a docile lamb accepting every suggestion Kris made. For now, they worked together in a fragile peace, avoiding discussing why the metal box got buried in sawdust or why its missing numbers weren't added. They worked hard at moving forward.

Without knowing why, Mom was thrilled with the improved atmosphere. "I know we'll have a wonderful season," she said, whipping up Kris's favorite cranberry-orange scones and every other treat that might tempt him.

He groaned. "Mom, I'll be fat in two weeks."

"Impossible. Look at you, all muscle, even after working at a desk in New York City. Here, eat this last scone."

"You forced me!" He chuckled but finished every crumb before loading up to drive into town to return the paint sprayer early enough to pay only one day's rental.

"What's that contraption?" Mom asked as he finished loading. He had scrubbed the telltale red paint from his hands.

"Equipment I rented for a repair."

"Oh? I didn't notice you using it."

Thankfully she didn't ask anything more. Today was Tuesday,

and Guthrie was leaning on him hard. He wanted an answer by Wednesday night. Tomorrow. Back home, Kris hammered Dad's financials into what should be a survivable plan through Christmas. Of course, he'd rather go large by growing the winning national tree. There was no payment, but national interest would pull orders pour in. Possibly for the Halvorsens, too, if they'd enter the competitions.

May the best man win! *Or woman,* he added, picturing Marcie in her cute forest green slacks and jacket.

Halvor's troubles had hit her hard, probably leaving her cautious and confused instead of full of her usual can-do fire. Plus, she was overwhelmed. He would take steps forward for the good of his family, whether Marcie had the courage to go forward or not.

Since when had Kris ever given up easily? Taken "no" for an answer before exhausting all options?

Seamus O'Leary. He must talk to him again and remind him that Wisconsin trees were a great choice. Besides, Seamus knew the status of many Christmas tree programs far beyond the Rockefeller Center. Did he still have O'Leary's phone number? Kris searched his worn billfold and the side pocket where he kept a small photo of Mom and Dad. Also one Laura Guthrie had given him of them attending a merger banquet. Beneath it, he found an old, dog-eared school photo of Marcie he'd forgotten he had.

He shook his head. Marcie was spunky. He hoped she would apply. Finally, under the photos, he found O'Leary's phone number on a scrap of paper. First thing tomorrow, he'd give the Irishman a call.

20

____

Seamus answered on the first ring.

"It's raining here. I'm actually sitting at my desk," the cheery fellow roared in his musical brogue. He'd been in America twenty years, but his speech still sang with Old Country charm. "You're phoning me from Christmas tree land? That's grand! You're making me jealous, lad. I should come see for myself."

"That's why I'm calling. You have a standing invitation. Mom would cook tasty Irish foods. The world needs to see our perfect evergreens and wonderful people. Your Rockefeller viewers will tire of seeing the same kind of tree every season."

"They might at that."

"Give us a try."

Seamus crowed. "Well done, me boy. You've nearly convinced me. We've locked in our choice with Ottawa, Canada for this year, but, saints preserve us, you're on my list for next year. Send me a detailed proposal. I'll pitch you to our organizers."

"Great, Seamus. Thanks. Meanwhile, if anything about this year's choice falls through, I'll get you a great one."

"Ho, ho. You don't give up, do you? Which is what I like in enterprising young men. Smart student!"

"Smart teacher," Kris quipped. "I know you also stay aware of other national displays and rub elbows with those decision-makers. Do you have updates?"

"I don't literally rub shoulders. Let's say when we meet at major events, we lift a glass together and talk. They're favoring Norway spruce again, much less fond of pine or fir. We know about the blight. How are you doing, Kris? Keeping your head up?"

"Yes. I'm looking up."

"Haha, best be careful, then, in case a bird flies over." He laughed again at his own joke.

"I have news about the National tree on the President's Park. Conservationists are pressuring them. They've used the same living tree for two years now and hope it lasts a third, but there's no guarantee. Now they call it the Capitol Christmas Tree or The People's Tree."

"Wow, that gives the tree national importance."

"Yes. The present one has wind and root damage. You'd be smart to send pictures of your trees soon as a beautiful replacement in case this one fails."

"Brilliant. Who would I contact?"

"It'll take me a minute to find that. They plan to choose specimens from across the US for the White House tree. Early ones came from the East Coast and then the West. I hear they're starting to look at the Midwest. You might be right on time."

"Winning to provide one out of three trees wouldn't be bad. I'll knock on every door to make them consider us."

"Good man," Seamus chuckled. "I tell you what. You're a smart lad and helped me understand the stock market."

"All legal information."

"I've made gains and appreciate it. Let me give the Washington D.C. contact your name and tell him you'll be in touch."

"That would be outstanding, Seamus."

"It should help. Your tree would have to meet all criteria, but applying early should give you an advantage."

"I appreciate it. When the world sees the trees we grow here, they'll want them for sure."

"And maybe the young men, too, I'm thinking. Once you're back, find me. We'll grab a meal and chat. I'd like to visit your area, but only when you're there to guide me."

"We'll do that. My folks will love you."

"By the way, there's a photo of your girlfriend with an up-and-coming young fellow splashed across the Society section of today's New York Times. Attending some other company acquisition function."

Kris stiffened. "She's not my girlfriend."

"No? When I saw you together, she hung on you like glue. In my country, that means something."

"Her dad had me take her. And then I invited her to dinner a few times after to say thanks."

"Girls draw conclusions. I see her around often. She's nice but spoiled."

"The danger of privilege. She calls me up wanting to go out more, but her dad keeps me so busy. Now I'm in Wisconsin."

"Well, if you're interested at all, you'd best step up. Just a minute while I find that headline."

Desk drawers opened and closed. Papers rattled.

"Here we go. 'Guthrie officer and heiress hit New York society. Is this a new power couple? These names could lead the company forward.'" Seamus rattled the paper again. "They *look* like a couple in the picture. She's draped over him."

Kris swallowed. "Does it give his name?"

"Johnson Elliott. Do you know him?"

"Yeah. He's the son of Guthrie's college roommate. A good-looking guy who wants to join the company. He made it clear he intends to make a big splash."

"Frankly, Rockefeller Center is crowded with fellows like that. They hang around, hoping to be discovered. Can't say from this photo—news gets skewed—but I'd say you have competition."

Kris tensed. "I'm not sure I care. I wasn't pursuing her, but before the opportunity passes me by, I guess I should decide."

"I'd say so. When are you coming back anyway?"

"Ten more days. Except Guthrie wants me back sooner."

"I don't blame him. Near as I can tell, you're his hardest working young officer. You're going places. Ah, well—I'll let you sort out your girl problems. Just glad I'm past that age. It makes me wish I had a daughter to introduce you to. Oh, I do have a niece ..."

Kris cleared his throat. "Uh—that's okay for now, Seamus. I'm sure she's great, but I'm busy. My life is complicated enough."

"Hold on! I just found the contact information for the Washington D.C. tree entries. Do you want to copy it down?"

"Yes, sir. Read away." Kris wrote furiously as he rattled off the number. "Thanks, Seamus. Now I can move forward."

"Good man. Nice talking with you."

An hour later, Kris had a solid plan. He'd give Marcie one last chance to enter the competitions. If she didn't? Well, he had made the offer. Shoulders back and head high, Kris walked through the long rows of beautiful trees on both properties, Marmaduke happily trotting alongside. Some trees in the Halvorsen Norway spruce rows showed healthy growth with green tips. Maybe their problem wasn't as widespread as they first thought. Kris whistled and then burst into song. "'O Tannenbaum, O Tannenbaum, how lovely are thy branches!'" Marmaduke howled in tune.

They sang loud enough that Dad joined in from several acres over, making Kris laugh and Duke bark harder.

Kris snapped his fingers. By working hard and asking God's blessing, they would bulldoze this mountain-sized problem down until even its dust blew away. Sure, they needed sales, but those would come. They could expect a great season!

21

Marcie spent her first two morning hours balancing their order list of tree sales with needed amounts of twine, netting, and tags, along with money in the bank. Barring her uncle's medical costs, they might scrape by. Sometimes, the local hardware store gave tree farmers ninety days to pay instead of the normal sixty during the considerable stretch of the Christmas sales season. Stores outside of Balsam weren't as flexible.

Task completed, Marcie fueled the garden tractor and attached its wagon to go to the brilliant red shed. She'd grab tools there to mark the first trees to be harvested and test her skills at trimming away blight.

The shed's transformation was so blazing it hurt her eyes. Ideally, that brilliant red was how all farm sheds and barns should look. Aunt Ingrid would love it. Marcie wasn't as sure about Uncle Halvor. There was no way yet to know how long he'd be out of commission. She'd plan on organizing and managing this season's work alone. If willing but untrained men from church did help, it would be hard to postpone her tasks to train and supervise. If Kris were around to guide them, that would ease the load. Otherwise, it was often easier to just do the work herself.

What was Kris up to? Maybe she upset him by not making an instant decision about the tree competitions. There was too much going on, too many balls in the air. Would she see him again during his time here? It sounded like his days might get cut short. He'd better figure out his status with the boss's daughter. He seemed genuinely embarrassed when his employer tracked him down at her house to talk to Kris by phone.

Marcie's faithful tractor put-putted. As she came closer, the red shed did look like flames. Moving flames! She shaded her eyes and saw activity along its roofline. Was the shed on fire? She shifted her tractor into high gear and sped near and then killed the engine. In the quiet, she heard a man shouting and a dog barking.

Instead of moving flames, it was a man in a red shirt swinging back and forth across the shed's roofline but dangling upside down. Below him, a dog mournfully howled and then ran and leaped up on Marcie, almost knocking her flat. It was the Lundquists' dog. Kris's dog.

"Marmaduke! What are you doing here?" Then the man was

...

She ran around the building and didn't know whether to feel distressed or amused.

"Kris! In the name of all that's sane, what are you doing up there, dangling above our shed?"

His face flushed redder than his shirt.

"You tell me. Get me down. It wasn't my idea. Did your uncle make a death trap for trespassers? A revenge machine?"

"What are you talking about?"

She stepped closer and saw.

"Now I get what happened, but it's just so—" She tried not to smirk but then, seeing he was not at immediate risk of death, she bent double, laughing, while Marmaduke licked her face, neck, and hands. She couldn't stop, and Duke didn't either.

"Don't leave me up here," Kris called. "Get me down. Duke, leave her alone."

"Kris, are you hurt?" She reduced her laughter to giggles. "You caught your foot in Uncle Halvor's coyote snare, and it jerked you upside down into the tree."

"Of course I did."

He didn't look amused.

"I hope you're not hurt."

"My leg is twisted, but my pride hurts worse." He looked around. "But the view is terrific." His swinging face wore a hint of a smile.

She scrambled up the ladder rungs on the building's side and reached the rope. She whipped out the utility knife on her belt and got ready to cut.

"Hold onto the roofline so you don't fall when I cut this."

"Good idea."

The sliced rope's edges fell. Kris inched his way down the ladder rungs, hand over hand until he reached the ground, and then rubbed his leg. Marcie's hands dropped to her hips.

"What were you doing up there anyway? Thinking up ways to calm down the bright paint? I have to admit, it looks good."

"Really?" He looked pleased. "I'm glad. Do you see where I'm standing? By the eavestrough over the rain barrel. I got the final information today about providing trees for Washington D.C. and maybe even the Rockefeller Center after all."

"You were putting that information on the shed roof?"

"No."

"What then?" She couldn't read his look.

"I wanted to put it in that plastic container we used to put messages in over the rain barrel but wired to the eavestrough. I hoped you'd find it and know we were still friends."

"We are. But what if I didn't find it? It's not like I look there often."

"Then, I would have waited a day and dropped scavenger

hunt clues. Or phoned you." He massaged his sore leg again but produced a grin.

"You're a hoot. None of those methods are direct. What about just crossing the road and dropping it by?" She giggled. "Underneath your New York City sophistication, you're the same nice, funny guy from years back. I wish I had a camera."

"I'm glad you don't." He blew out an exaggerated breath. "We were close friends that summer."

"The best. Now, if you've recovered, I have tons of work to do. I'll climb up and get your information to read later."

"No. I hand-deliver."

He climbed stiffly, wincing, but presented the papers with a flourish.

"Here you are, Miss Halvorsen. Please consider my invitation to enter the competitions to save our farms and make Wisconsin Christmas trees famous across America. I await your decision. If you enter, maybe we can ship our trees together."

He ended with a bow.

She clapped. "Bravo. Very gentlemanly. You'll have my answer tomorrow."

Limping slightly, Kris recrossed the property line back onto Lundquist land.

As he passed through tree rows to resume his chores, Mom rang the porch bell for lunch. She didn't work today?

He checked his watch. Noon already? Morgan Guthrie would be phoning for his answer. Kris sped to the house as fast as his leg allowed. When the phone did ring several minutes later, he gulped a breath and answered.

"Mr. Guthrie. Yes, fine, thanks. How are things there?"

His employer's voice growled through the phone. "Kristopher, they'd go better if you'd get back here where you belong. I left a board meeting to make this call. Don't disappoint me. Give me the answer I want. I took the liberty of looking at flights. I have one in your name on my charge card for Friday morning. Your other choice is Monday, but that's the absolute latest. I'm being generous to consider that much time."

Kris paused.

"Kris? Are you there? Have we lost the connection?" Something rattled or shook. "Stupid phones!"

"I'm here, Mr. Guthrie. I'm still considering. I hope you know how much I enjoy working with you. I've learned more in two years than in my business courses and master's degree altogether."

"I'm sure of that."

Kris held up a hand for Mom to quiet the clattering dishes and silverware she brought to the table.

"You're the most promising young man I've had for some time. And my personal grease monkey," he chuckled. "But I need to know where your loyalties lie."

"Sir? What if I commit four hours of prime business time daily to be available by phone for my remaining days here? Then could I complete the full two weeks?"

"Don't split hairs. I shouldn't have agreed to that much time off in the first place. It was unwise of you to ask. I have great things in mind for you, but it's important to forge ahead and seize the moment now. Things are happening. Opportunities don't wait. We're leaders, not followers."

"I agree, sir."

"Then I can count on you being here Friday or Monday?"

"I don't know yet." Kris's gut twisted. "Could my commitment of four prime time hours daily allow me the full two weeks?"

Kris heard a strange sound on Guthrie's end.

"Do you know what you're asking? You have strong skills, but I expect loyalty. I reward key men well. I brought you to my home, set you up with Laura to squire a major event, and you've connected other times. She likes you, Kris. That should mean something. I'm sure you see the advantages of such a connection. But I won't have her sitting home idle while you're away doing small-town things."

"I understand, sir."

"I wonder if you do. Important things happen in the Big Apple every day. She needed to be seen at this big merger event. You weren't here, so I sent her with a good-looking young man eager to join our firm. He's not as talented as you but comes from good social circles. Plus, he was available. You were not. Their picture is in today's papers."

Kris gulped. "I understand."

"I'm laying it out plain. I'd like you back Friday. If you're not here by Monday, you won't like what I will tell you then."

"Mr. Guthrie? I appreciate your call. Please tell Laura hello for me."

"If she matters, phone her yourself. Unless you're too busy saving a small-time Christmas tree operation."

"There's more involved than you think. It belongs to my family."

"See you soon, Lundquist." The connection ended.

Kris's head swam. Guthrie had pummeled him with velvet gloves. He might have lost his job. It should hurt worse than this, but he still felt numb.

"What was all that about?" Mom asked.

"My boss in New York. He'd approved my request for two weeks home, but now fresh opportunities have come up, so he gave me an ultimatum. Return Friday or Monday at the latest, or else."

Dad walked in from washing up for lunch. "Or else what? What did you tell him?"

"He wouldn't consider my offer of four hours of prime phone time daily from here. I don't see the issue like he does, but he's serious. I need to consider carefully. Many young MBA grads would jump at my opportunity."

Dishing up mashed potatoes, spoon still mid-air, Mom paused. "But you're entitled to a life of your own."

"I thought so."

"What will he do?"

"I'm not sure, but he's giving broad hints. He won't accept a reasonable compromise. He's jerking me hard on a short rope."

"That sounds a bit like a cattle sale," Dad said.

Kris snorted. "Sadly, no. It's high-stakes Human Resources." He waved a hand. "Sorry, Mom. Your food looks great, but I can't eat right now. Please save me a plate."

"Tough employer." She rested a hand on Kris's shoulder. "I'm not sure I want you back there if you're not appreciated enough, but if you have to cut your time short, we understand."

"You've already done wonders to help us," Dad said. "I'll try hard to keep my head screwed on straight from here on."

Kris passed a weary hand through his hair and dropped his shoulders. "It's not only your needs I care about. I'm not quite ready to go back. Not so sure New York is the place I want to spend that much energy. It's not only finances. All the end results have to count."

He climbed the steps to his room, still shaking his head.

22

Marcie sailed through her chores faster than she thought. By day's end, she still smiled whenever she pictured Kris's antics. What a guy. One of a kind. Recalling him dangling from the tree snare made her laugh out loud. That photo would be worth a fortune. He'd succeed in New York or wherever his gifts took him. It was a shame a talented businessman couldn't thrive in Balsam. With hard work, she hoped to be an exception to make her seedling and tree nursery succeed.

Kris was sweet to pass on the national tree competition information. He could have just kept it to himself, but he'd always been kind during the years she'd known him except for that teenage phase when he was a big tease.

A year after moving to Halvor and Ingrid's, she'd roamed the woods gathering wildflowers for Mom's grave when she found a rabbit caught in a snare, leg broken. She had screamed, trying to release it, and Kris had come running. That's how they'd met. As quick as anything, he managed what she couldn't and freed the hurting animal. When he carried it to his Dad's packing shed to make a brace and set the leg with a stick and tape, she followed.

She visited during the weeks it was healing and was there the day he released it for a long, happy bunny life in the woods. She figured it had grandbunnies by now.

No matter what New York tried to make of Kris, she was glad to see his gentleness and kindness remain intact.

Ingrid hadn't phoned. Halvor's reports must have been delayed, but Marcie knew her aunt would reach her with anything urgent. The sun had set, and Marcie stifled a yawn heading for bed when the phone rang again.

"Marcie? This is Lisa from the bank. I hope I'm not phoning too late."

"Dave's Lisa? No, I'm up. How are you?"

"Fine. I'm sorry to bother you with your uncle ill. I want him to do well and know he needs time to recover, but my boss insisted I call. You probably know we've been sending Halvor letters about getting significant payment to us on what he owes by the end of the year."

"I don't know the details, but he mentioned something."

"I'm sorry he's sick. Dave and I are praying he'll have a quick recovery, but my boss is wondering if Halvor has plans to take care of the debt."

Marcie gasped. "He wants to know that right now? Halvor said something. Ingrid may know more. I just got home from university but will try to find out." She paused. "The bank president asked you to phone tonight?"

"Yes. I'm sorry. I almost told him no, but he insisted. Now I wish I had refused. I'll tell him so in the morning."

"My uncle has volunteered on many town projects with him, but it's all right, Lisa. I understand. You're in a hard place."

"Not as hard as you. I wish I'd looked into this detail before I called. I believe the bank sometimes has a clause to defer payment when the head of household is ill. At least for a while. I'll research that more tomorrow."

Marcie released the breath she hadn't realized she'd been holding. "We would appreciate that. That would be a great encouragement for Halvor and Ingrid. They're facing so many unknowns."

"Thanks for being gracious. Now, if you're not ready to shoot me for my first question, here's my second."

Marcie hesitated. "Go on. I think I'm ready."

"It won't be long until Balsam Days when we celebrate our founding days, dress up like early characters, and re-enact major events."

"I guess that is coming up fast. I love that weekend."

"If you remember, each year there's a parade, with Miss Balsam riding with the mayor in a Christmas sleigh up front. Some of us on that committee were kicking ideas around. We came up with a name the mayor likes."

"What's that got to do with me?"

"Everything. We want you to be Miss Balsam."

23

Kris never took mid-day naps. They made him groggy. But he'd been exhausted from swinging upside-down like an acrobat in that ridiculous snare over the Halvorsen shed and had fallen asleep on his bed. He pictured Marcie's face, laughing, trying to figure how he got up there and how to get him down. He was glad she hadn't had a camera.

He'd forgotten his boss's phone call until his head emerged a little more fully from sleep, and suddenly Guthrie's face swam into view. Then Laura's. Whoops. Things did not end well. He needed to communicate clearly without giving in. But if he did buckle and go back, where would that path lead in ten years? Or twenty? He might possess impressive power and finances. But was that all he wanted?

Kris didn't think Guthrie himself was happy. When he had fixed the problem on his boss's Porsche, the man said, "When I was young, I loved fast cars. Racing. Doing mechanic repairs. Grease under my nails. I thought that's what I would do for a living."

"What happened?"

"I got serious with Miranda and wanted to marry her. Her dad wanted something solid for her, a husband with a richer future. He offered me a spot in his business, and I had a knack for it. My career's gone straight up since then, no complaints there. Back in high school, I would have washed cars for a week to ride in a Porsche. Now I own one. Still, I sometimes wonder what life would have been like if I'd taken the other road."

"Do you have regrets?"

"No regrets. I just wonder sometimes."

Kris wondered, too. The Porsche dealers in New York City earned a good income. The mechanics worked long hours but were paid well.

And then Kris pictured Laura. He'd met the young man who had squired her this week. Laura was high society. She always looked like a glossy fashion magazine cover. How would she do if she ever hit hard times? He'd been so busy working on Dad's mess. He should at least give her a friendly call.

Next, he pictured Marcie's laughing face, upside down while he dangled. That hadn't been fun, but it made a great memory.

He didn't remember exactly when she and her mom moved to Halvor and Ingrid's. He didn't notice her until that summer when he had heard cries for help. She'd found an injured rabbit in a snare and wanted to save it. She was small but feisty, crying buckets from eyes that also held compassion and fire. He'd splinted the bunny and cared for it. She'd visited several times before it healed enough to be let go and seemed grateful. He'd forgotten that that was a year after her mother's death. The poor kid had suffered a lot.

She still fought for causes she championed. Right now, that meant Halvor and Ingrid. She was the bright silver lining in their cloud. She was the kind of gal anyone would want on their team. But what was he thinking? He had to make the rest of today count for work here on Dad's place.

He sat up and swung his feet to the floor. Maybe he could eat something now before heading to the fields. He thought about Marcie again. They'd been an item one summer the year before he'd graduated. He'd surprised her by carving their initials together in a heart on one of the biggest trees. They'd *gone steady* until it fell apart during his senior year. He never really understood why. He wondered if he could find that tree and the carved heart now. Or if bark had grown over it. He'd look for it one day soon.

If anything, Marcie was more attractive and fascinating today than years ago. Now spruce blight and sales challenges gave fresh reasons to spend time together. He hoped she would enter at least one of the tree competitions. He had savings and a few investments to fall back on to help Dad. He didn't think Halvor did. Kris also had a regular paycheck as long as his job lasted. At least, he hoped he still had a job.

24

Marcie knew chances for winning any competition were incredibly small. Kris had been clear about that. But even entering made their farms better known regionally and nationally, so that alone was worth the effort

She loved Balsam—population 1924, until the next baby was born—but she'd need a broader base to get her silviculture seed and conifer seedling nursery started. To succeed, Halvorsen Farms needed to be respected and widely known.

Her top professor had studied in England and loved pithy British sayings. His favorite was, 'In for a penny, in for a pound,' which originally meant if you borrowed a penny to start a business, you might as well borrow and invest a full pound to do it right.

That phrase fit. She would go large and enter both national contests alongside Kris. Chances were small, but one of them might win. Whatever happened, both farms would become better known.

Her excitement grew. Yes, she'd apply to provide trees for both projects. Their own farm had those two gorgeous sentinels at the end of the driveway, untouched by disease. They were

Balsam fir. She didn't know if that variety was acceptable this year or not. If the Rockefeller entry were a possibility, she'd enter that, too.

She squared her shoulders. Kris was right. You'd never get anywhere if you didn't knock on doors and ask. If not this year, the next. Or the year after. Even navigating the application process should expand their business opportunities. The next time she was in Madison and saw that professor, she'd tell him that 'in for a penny, in for a pound' also worked fine with Christmas trees.

She couldn't wait to tell Kris but wouldn't inform Ingrid and Halvor yet. Or perhaps not at all. They were trusting farm management to her for now. She'd let them know if they placed in the finals. Then they would wildly celebrate.

Why hadn't Ingrid phoned tonight with updates on more test results? Things were probably delayed. Still, Marcie would feel better hearing some word.

Her time with her aunt yesterday had been unforgettable.

"Halvor was so shocked," Ingrid said, "when he realized his dad had the same stroke pattern but died. I think that scared him enough to cooperate."

"I'll bet. And to trust the Lord." Marcie searched for the best way to express everything in her heart. "I hope you know I'll always do all I can to help you two." She cleared her throat and looked into Ingrid's eyes. "Please don't worry."

Her aunt took her in her arms.

"Dear heart. A little worry won't hurt me. But if there's anything I know, it is that you always do your best for us. Probably more than you should. We're so connected by love, and we can't imagine our lives without you. Please know what you mean to us and how you bless us with liveliness and laughter. We thank God for you constantly."

Love washed over Marcie like soothing ointment. As Ingrid's gentle eyes filled with tears, so did hers.

"Well, aren't we a soggy mess," Marcie said after several seconds. And they hugged and laughed again.

Marcie's warm remembrances were interrupted by the phone ringing, and she lunged for it eagerly. But it wasn't Ingrid. Instead, it was a female voice Marcie had not heard before, demanding to speak to Kris Lundquist.

"Kris Lundquist? No, he's not here. Should he be?"

"He was last time." The jarring voice had a nasal twang. From watching television, Marcie pegged the speaker as a New Yorker.

"My faw-ther reached Kris at this number."

"Excuse me?" Marcie snapped to attention. "Who is calling?"

"Kris hasn't called me, so I'm investigating. I want to know who you are and what you're up to. He talked to Dad from this number, so you must be part of what's keeping him there. It's not fair. He's needed here. Give him my message."

Marcie held the phone away from her ear. The voice was commanding.

"Just a minute. You've phoned a private residence. We're neighbors to the Lundquists but not involved in their business and don't provide message service. My uncle is in a health crisis, and this line must stay open for hospital calls. I'm hanging up now."

"No!" The voice became strident. "I'll warn you, I usually get what I want. It doesn't go well for people who don't help me. Tell Kris to call now."

"Are you threatening me?" Marcie's voice honed to knife-edge sharpness. "Let me tell you, miss whoever-you-are, we don't live or work that way in Wisconsin. I don't interfere in Kris's life and hope you won't. I will not cooperate with you. Don't call here again!"

She slammed the receiver down so hard it rang, and the glimpse of her face in the living room mirror cheered her. Warlike. Determined. A face that might belong on Mount Rushmore.

Well, that put a spring in her step. Her skin tingled. Maybe she could overcome any challenge.

She would not tell Kris about this call unless tortured. She doubted little miss boss's daughter would either. Kris would be wise to avoid her clutches. And if that gal ever came to Wisconsin, well, she'd soon learn Midwestern women were a force to be reckoned with.

25

Kris had forgotten that Balsam Days on the first weekend in November kicked off Christmas season. He had answered Morgan Guthrie's ultimatum with his own via telegram.

"I appreciate and respect you. Our family's tree operation is small but vital. Without sharing details, I need more time, not less. Will be away a month, maybe more. If you can hold my job, great. If not, this is still something I must do."

The answering telegram said, "Keenly disappointed. You are a skilled asset. I'd like you back on any terms but no Christmas bonus. Pay your own airfare. Wire if coming. If not, your office goes to Johnson Elliott on January 1st."

Fair enough, Kris thought. *That probably includes Laura, too.* He found he did not mind.

He had not heard Marcie would be Miss Balsam, heading the parade with the mayor in a Christmas sleigh. She looked perfect there. Smiling. Waving. Tossing candies to kids along the parade route.

His heart swelled. Knowing the townspeople and seeing them pull together made this more meaningful than Macy's world-famous televised Thanksgiving Day Parade.

He'd rather be here where marching bands blasted trumpets and twirled sticks between drumming out their stirring beats. He'd been a drummer in school and felt the powerful rhythms now. If he had a son or daughter and could support himself here, he'd like them to be part of this one day.

What was he thinking? That wasn't realistic. But wherever he heard them, powerful marching bands stirred his heart to patriotism every time. It did again today. The brass instruments and tubas, too, with a young high school majorette tossing her twirling baton into the air.

Everyone in town turned out. Every kid wanted their turn marching someday. He'd had his day and been just as proud.

Leading the parade with the mayor in the Lundquists' splendid, decorated sleigh, Marcie perfectly fulfilled Miss Balsam. Standing upright, in a fabulous forest green velvet sheath dress with matching gloves that made her a very graceful tree, her radiant smile was the greatest beauty of all.

Sparkling stones graced the diadem on her head, flashed around her throat, dazzled from the bracelets on both wrists, and twinkled from her ears. The adornments looked like gorgeous snowflakes and gleaming icicles beautifying the evergreen's branches. Everything about her was perfect, but she was lovely herself. She didn't need greater beautifying.

For a moment, Kris's mind flashed to Laura. Her beauty had been static, the two-dimensional glossy magazine cover type that faded with time. Marcie's was living three-dimensional, the real thing that coped with good or bad situations just the same and steadily rose like cream to the top.

Ingrid waved to her from the curb, Halvor beside her. He was in a wheelchair, but back in Balsam for the first time since his stroke. After transitional steps tried his patience but aided his recovery, his face was more lined but serene. He still idolized his forefathers, but seeing the man's perseverance made Kris swallow the lump in his throat. He was sure Halvor's forefathers would be equally proud of him. Ingrid beamed at her husband and niece.

Kris had found a note from Marcy in the plastic container above the shed's eavestrough mail container. Their communication system was back in operation, but he'd learned to avoid the snare. After both sent in paperwork applications to provide trees for all three national opportunities, they'd heard back and were among the top five entries for the White House tree.

After today's parade, they would meet together to hammer out details to coordinate their first big tree harvest of this season. They could score significant savings by coordinating shipping to Twin Cities locations.

For Balsam Days only, Hudson's fabulous ice cream shoppe had set up a portable restaurant. Lisa Scholz operated a cookie stand right next to it. Both enjoyed brisk sales.

"Cookies and ice cream go great together," Lisa said as Kris and Marcie walked past.

"I'll buy a dozen each of snickerdoodles and peppermint crunchies and two dozen of your Christmas tree shapes with sprinkles. I'll mail those tomorrow to my buddy Seamus at Rockefeller Center as part of my campaign to get him out here."

"Sounds great. Thanks for your business." Lisa sealed the bag with a flourish. "Glad to see your uncle here, Marcie. How's he doing?"

"Making slow but steady progress. The church work parties helped us so much. He couldn't believe the improvements and repairs, especially in the shipping shed. Once he swallowed his pride, he was so relieved to see tasks under control. When you found he qualified for an extension on the loan due date without penalty—well, that was frosting on the cake."

"I'm happy, too."

The women shared warm smiles before Lisa returned to her long line of customers.

Kris and Marcie slipped into the ice cream shoppe and snagged two seats as a couple left.

"What's the Balsam special?" Marcie asked the waitress.

"A chocolate fudge brownie shaped like a tree log in a dish with mounded green peppermint mint ice cream on both sides and small colorful candy balls sprinkles on top. Plus, we have a contest where people can suggest their creations. The winner will have their sundae named after them. Every time one is sold, five cents goes to their favorite charity."

"Wonderful." Kris accepted a sample spoonful. "I've got to meet whoever thought up this idea. He's brilliant."

"He's my husband," the waitress said. "Come back later when things slow down, and I'll arrange it." She opened her order pad. "Now, what will you have?"

"Definitely the yule log," Kris said.

"Make it two."

The waitress nodded, snapped her pad closed, and bustled off. Kris turned to Marcie.

"So, is your Uncle Halvor okay with you eating ice cream with me here?"

"Maybe not delighted. After all, he's still Norwegian, and you're not, but he knows many here have done wonders to keep us going, and you played a key part. He asked why you haven't returned to New York City." She gazed into his eyes. "Are you going back?"

"Would you believe me if I said I don't know yet?"

"It's a huge decision. Anyway, I believe Uncle Halvor is humbled and changed by all that happened. Not perfect but changed."

"Good to hear. Depending on his health, maybe I'll swing by and visit him sometime."

Marcie hesitated. "Wait a week or so until he's more settled, and then that might be fine."

"I'll let you tell me when. Now, let me tell you what is working out for tree shipping for our first big cut. That's going to be our biggest savings in terms of sales. Harvesting and shipping together lets us minimize shipping and maximize profits."

"We're grateful."

"I'll cut and mesh twelve hundred trees. How many did you say you're doing?"

"Fifteen hundred to settle our remaining loan debt. It will take every bit of that. We have lots riding on this, so thanks for making it happen."

"Sure thing. These days, lots of people put up their trees at Thanksgiving or sooner. We'll have ours cut and delivered for those first sales, and might be the first ones on the market."

She smiled. "That gives me a huge sense of relief. First thing Saturday morning, then? We'll cut and have everything ready."

"Yes. On Saturday morning, trucks will roll."

"You're sure everything will work out? Once the trees are cut and trimmed, there's no going back."

"Guaranteed." He took her hand. "I'm sure of my contacts. Everything will be fine. It's good our farms are next to each other, makes loading and transport easier."

"Thank Goodness, three high school boys on our road need extra money. They'll start cutting right after school Friday."

"Perfect. We're paying some men from church raising funds for the senior housing project."

They worked out details while finishing their ice cream.

Axes and chain saws rang all Friday afternoon and evening. They began again at sun-up. Both farms had their trees bundled in mesh and piled in neat stacks by the roadside early Saturday, ready for pick-up.

"Good morning, Marcie," Kris called cheerfully across the road.

"Good morning yourself. Any sign of the trucks?"

"They should be here any minute." He checked notes on his clipboard. "They were scheduled to leave their depot at 7:30 a.m. sharp to get here by 9 a.m. It's about that now."

They checked trees and waited. And waited some more.

Halvor watched through the house window. Ingrid came out and stood on the porch. "Is everything all right?" she called. "We're wondering why we don't see the trucks. Have you heard anything?"

Kris searched the road, ready to hear sounds of delayed trucks rolling in.

"Not yet, and I don't understand. They guaranteed today's date and delivery time to the Twin Cities."

"It's important, Kris," Marcie felt her face tighten. "Would you please check to be sure everything is all right?"

"Sure. I'll be right back."

He loped up the drive to his house and disappeared inside to phone. Five minutes passed and then ten. Finally, he reappeared, head down, slowly walking to the road. Lars and Karin followed.

"What's wrong?" Marcie called before they arrived.

"You won't believe it. I don't believe it myself. But if it's the last thing I do, I'll fix this. We will not fail."

"Okay, just tell us what happened." Marcie's face was pasty white. Ingrid's looked the same. With effort, Halvor made his way to the porch. The rest of their families stood in a knot on opposite sides of the road.

"The head office got a call yesterday changing the address for where the trucks should go. They sent them two hours south by mistake and have no more trucks available."

Kris looked up.

"By any chance, did anyone at your place do that?"

People in both groups looked at each other. Everyone shook their head. Marcie's hands flared to her hips. "Seriously, Kris. How could we? We didn't know the trucking company's name or phone number. I guess we should have."

"That would have been easy to get from Information," Lars mumbled. His wife jabbed him. "Lars! Stop."

"Only if we knew what to ask for," Marcie said, "and we didn't. We left it in your hands."

Kris's head dropped. "I know. It's awful, but I'll fix this somehow."

"We need the money from these trees," Marcie's voice shook.

"If we don't get it, we're done. My university advisor phoned, offering me a research job at good pay in Madison. I turned him down. I want to live here, but I may have to reconsider."

"No!" Her words were knives scraping Kris's throat. "Don't do that. That's the last thing I want."

"We can't always do what we want. Sometimes we have to do what helps our family."

Kris gritted his teeth. "There's an answer, and I'll find it."

Ingrid crossed the road and placed a hand on his shoulder. "It's hard to know what went wrong and doesn't matter. Something did, and it affects us all. If our trees dry out, we can't survive that loss. We'd best go home and pray. That's the only way we'll get answers."

"You're right, Ingrid. Thank you. When I have a solution, I'll let you know."

26

"Tell me again what happened," Kris repeated on the phone, his voice rising. "Who called in the cancellation? Not a cancellation? Someone changed where the trucks should go? Yes, we're the Lundquists in Balsam, but none of us called you. Please check again. We need to know what happened."

Several minutes passed before the dispatcher came back on the line.

"Mr. Lundquist, we're terribly sorry. Our regular gal is out for surgery, and the new secretary doesn't know our customers. We also serve a client named Lindquist, spelled almost the same. They needed one truck two hours south. Our replacement gal thought it was the same name, different address, and sent your trucks to them. Their truck should have come to you but threw an engine rod, so it's out of commission. We can't do anything this weekend. Our trucks are fully scheduled next Monday through Friday. We'll give you a huge discount next time you ship with us."

"That's not enough and doesn't do us any good now." Kris made an inarticulate sound and hung up. Mom and Dad sat with their heads bowed. After an emergency prayer of his own, ideas began coming. Kris kept his notepad, pen, and phone busy for the next two hours.

Around noon, he walked to the Halvorsens' place. When he knocked, Marcie opened the door red-eyed. Across the room, Halvor sat in his wheelchair, expressionless. Marcie left the door open but stepped outside.

"Let's talk here."

Kris clutched his clipboard and jammed his free hand into his pocket.

"Listen," he stumbled, "I can't say how bad I feel. Sometime I'll explain how the company confused Lundquist with Lindquist and sent trucks to the wrong place. Anyhow, as we prayed, ideas came. I called in some contact favors. It's a patched-together system of farm trucks and rail cars that cross the tracks below our hill. It means lots of work. The trucks will ferry our trees to the rail cars to load as soon as the train stops. They'll rush our trees to the Twin Cities, short and sweet."

Marcie's face slowly brightened. "Amazing. That all happens today?"

"Yes, if we start now. Also, some people I talked to are impressed with our effort. They're doing radio and newspaper coverage about determined farmers getting their Christmas trees to market. People will come to see our trees arrive and buy even before they reach the sales lots."

"Seriously?"

"Yes, ma'am." He grinned.

"Well done, Kris," Halvor called through the open door. "Marcie, shake that young man's hand."

"Gladly," she said, and added a hug.

27

After enough worry to make Marcie want to pull out her hair, the Christmas tree delivery succeeded. Thanks to Kris's friends, shipping costs were low, so profits increased. Their second tree-cutting and shipment took place flawlessly. Halvor's remaining loan debt payments were paid up to date and slightly ahead. Marcie greeted officers at the bank and walked out with her head held high.

Some days, she burst into song as her aunt and uncle's health improved. Halvor walked with a walker as his bad leg started obeying. His weak arm strengthened, thanks to the rehab specialist who came to the house. He could open and close a fist but didn't need a fist as often. One day Marcie heard him singing, but he stopped when she poked her head through the door to see if she was hearing correctly.

It was good she collected the mail now because yesterday's delivery brought disappointment. After two qualifying rounds, The President's Park Christmas tree would not be from Wisconsin but a sixty-five-foot red fir provided by a California grower.

Today's official envelope came from the National Christmas Tree Association Committee postmarked Littleton, Colorado.

Strange, because she'd mailed that application to a Washington DC address as requested. She read their reply on the porch.

"Dear tree grower and NCTA member,

"Thank you for applying to supply this year's White House tree for display in the Blue Room. This year's tree will be decorated by our First Lady, Lady Bird Johnson. Starting this year, our organization will select the tree from the submissions of our member growers.

"We are excited to receive the description and photos of your magnificent Balsam fir. It meets our height and width requirements and has pleasing symmetry. In the judging process, your Halvorsen Farms entry ranks among the top five finalists. Final judging is underway. We will narrow the field to two top competitors and then do final judging to announce this year's winning supplier.

"Thank you for your membership and support of our organization. Growers like you honor our profession by growing the best Christmas trees in America. Congratulations as you move closer to being this year's top grower with the privilege of providing our White House tree.

"Sincerely, Bernard Hughes, NCTA President"

Marcie clamped a hand over her mouth so she wouldn't squeal and twirled in a circle. It was official. At the end of the first round, Halvorsen Farms was among the top five finalists in alphabetical order. Lundquist Farms was right below them. She wouldn't be here without Kris's help. What must he be thinking? Two of the nation's top five growers were neighbors in Wisconsin. In fact, they were friends. But only one could win.

She rushed inside. "Uncle Halvor? Aunt Ingrid? Don't worry, it's good news, but we need to talk."

28

Across the road, like a rerun of a popular movie, the same scenario took place in the Lundquist home. Kris showed his parents that they were the fourth name down of five—right under Halvorsen.

"I didn't want to raise your hopes until I knew we had a chance, but read this. We're in the top five finalists to provide this year's White House Christmas tree. Next, they'll narrow the entries to the top two. Several days after that, they'll announce a final decision."

"Seriously? How wonderful!" Mom leaned over to read the letter.

"The Halvorsens *and* us?" Dad asked. "What are the odds? That's nuts but outstanding. I guess we're meant to compete with them on everything. What else happens next?"

"More measurements, pictures, and judging. As I said, it gets narrowed down to two. Over the weekend, they'll announce the final selection Lady Bird Johnson will decorate. We can accompany the tree to D.C. if we want. Maybe even meet her."

"Gracious, I'd love it," Mom said.

"The final announcement and actual decorating both get full radio, TV, and news coverage to every home in America."

"And beyond," Mom exclaimed. "It doesn't get better than that. Lady Bird has such a gift for style. I love the way she beautifies our nation's roadways with wildflowers. She'll do something incredible with the tree, like use ornaments with the flowers and birds of each state."

"You're right," Lars agreed. "That would look terrific, plus it would be smart politics."

"She is one smart lady, and I'm thrilled we're this far." Kris refolded the letter and returned it to its envelope. "Marcie and I both applied to supply all three national trees. The one at President's Park, the White House, even Rockefeller Center if their tree from Canada falls through."

Lars beamed. "I'm glad to hear she entered. That seems like quite a stretch for her. Halvor and Ingrid must be bursting their buttons to also be in the top five. What a great way to get publicity."

"Thanks, Kris." Mom hugged him. "You're bringing our farm to a whole new level. Helping us reach solid footing."

"That's all I wanted, and it feels great." He hugged her back. "Be prepared, though. This means inspectors and photographers will hang around our place and the Halvorsens' constantly during this last stage. I'm glad their blight seems under better control. Get ready for news articles, magazine photos, radio and TV coverage—every kind of news and probably media people underfoot at all times."

"Bring it on." Lars clapped Kris's back. "Have you decided what you'll tell Guthrie about going back?"

Kris froze. "I almost forget to think about him. I'd better decide, so he hears from me instead of getting this tree award news another way."

"You're too late. We're there." Dad lifted the local paper brought in from the porch and tapped the headline, *Two local tree growers in nation's top five.* "Does that mean the story is already nationwide?"

"I'm afraid so." Kris scrubbed his face with his hands. "But it's just as well. Any attention helps us."

Mom grabbed a broom. "I'd better tidy the house before reporters arrive."

"Don't worry, Mom. You always keep things nice. It's like selling a house and keeping it ready for showings."

"That's right," Dad said. "I helped my dad sell a place once. Which reminds me, I'll go outside and check around. Spot things out of place and get them in order."

"Good man." Mom kissed his weathered cheek, and he pulled her close for a hug.

29

The award hubbub accelerated to high gear. White House Christmas tree finalist judges and reporters descended on both farms and the other locations across the U.S. The top two finalists would be notified by phone two days later at 6 p.m. That evening, the Lundquists and Halvorsens sat in their respective homes, waiting.

At 6 p.m., both phones rang.

Dignified voices at the end of both lines said, "Based on your tree's quality and appeal, your entry is one of our top two contenders. Next comes the final round with the strictest judging. For that, both trees will be cut and every inch examined. The winner goes to Washington D.C. The runner-up tree will be auctioned for a high price which the grower keeps. Congratulations and good luck. We will reach our decision soon. May the best tree win."

"May it be a Norwegian grower," Halvor muttered. Ingrid narrowed her eyes.

Across the road, Lars hoisted a fist in the air. "Winning would solve our problems."

Kris hesitated. "But we need what's best for all of us. We've already had national news coverage and free advertising. Coming this far is a big stride forward for the business."

Activity rose to fever pitch. Radio, TV, and newspaper reporters swarmed both farms like locusts, coming early and staying late. It was hard for both farms to get regular tree work done.

"I'm going to put you guys to work while you interview us," Kris told some newsmen. Several cooperated and gained feature stories about the family farms and tree cultivation.

Kris's mom added extra plates at their table for meals.

"How's Marcie holding up under this pressure?" she asked Kris during a quiet moment.

"I don't know. Haven't seen her."

"What? Why?" Mom waited.

He shrugged. "No good reason. Halvor's home and getting therapy. Marcie's working hard getting her next tree shipment cut and sold. Since we're both White House finalists, I figured I shouldn't bother her. Besides, reporters are always hanging around."

"Well, think again. Both being in the finals is a miracle. Checking on friends is a kindness, not a bother. It would be best to check in person to see how they're doing."

He stepped to the edge of the porch and gazed across the distance.

"You're right. I should."

He almost thought he saw Marcie's figure on their porch gazing back. If she were home, he'd rather see her in person than use the phone. He started walking. Why did he hear music each time he saw Marcie lately? A full symphony with sweeping violins. His heart constricted. What was happening to him? As he walked faster, his thoughts fell into place. For a hotshot financial advisor, why was he the last to know what he was thinking lately?

He was crazy about Marcie. She constantly filled his thoughts. He didn't want to go anywhere she wasn't or start any project without her. Forget New York and its trappings. Balsam with Marcie was home. Surely the problem with Halvor would lessen. Maybe it already was.

Kris stopped short. What if Marcie accepted the high-paying job in Madison and left him here? She wouldn't, would she? He couldn't let that happen. He didn't have a plan and wasn't ready, but his heart knew what it wanted. He squared his jaw and walked faster still, passing by the tree at the end of his driveway. The boughs were decorated with bright ornaments, and his eyes were caught by the loops on their tops. He snatched one and stuck it in his pocket, just in case. His pinky finger slipped reassuringly into its ring. It would have to do.

He gulped a breath and burst through the fringe of lilacs separating the yard from the Christmas tree rows. Marcie was on the front porch, all right, surrounded by newsmen with cameras and flashbulbs. Her aunt was there, too, distributing snacks.

Ingrid looked up. "Kris, nice to see you. Come get something to eat. How are you and your folks?"

"Hi, Ingrid, fine." But he looked at Marcie, willing her to look up. He sauntered forward, hands jammed in his pockets. "Just checking on you all. How's it going?"

"Busy but great," Ingrid said.

Marcie finally turned his way, but before she could speak, another newsman with a movie camera demanded, "Look this way, Miss Halvorsen. Angle your face toward the trees for an action shot. Good. Now, lift a hand to shade your eyes."

"Like this?"

"Perfect. Now give us your other side." He clicked away.

"Nice to see you, Lundquist," a different photographer called. "Get ready. We're heading to your place next."

"I'll head home and tell Mom." Kris gave a wave before turning and hurrying away.

30

After the fiasco of wanting to see Marcie but getting scared off by photographers, Kris buried himself in work. On the night before the final announcement, a journalist he'd befriended sidled up to him.

"Uh, Lundquist. You've been good to us while we've interrupted your lives. You've included us like part of your family."

Kris shook his hand. "You fit in well out here."

"I want to give you a tip I overheard. Wear your best shirt tomorrow and show your best side to the cameras."

Kris dropped what he was doing. "Why? What's up?"

"Your tree is going to the White House."

"You're sure? Not the Halvorsens'? Their Balsam fir is gorgeous, and they need the win."

"That has nothing to do with it. Winning depends on the tree, and the judges chose yours. Go see for yourself. They just wired on the preliminary tags while they're printing final award labels. Because of media frenzy, they're also moving up tomorrow's award time from noon to 9 a.m. Be there."

"Thanks. Will do. What an honor!"

"A once-in-a-lifetime event, unless you've learned enough skills to repeat a win."

"I doubt that." As soon as the journalist left, Kris's excitement faded. He still had limited investment savings to help his folks. And good prospects if he returned to New York. As far as he knew, the Halvorsens had nothing unless Marcie went to Madison. That must not happen!

He paced. And prayed. Twenty minutes later, he found his dad.

"Do me a favor. Come look at the tree entries with me."

"Sure, but it's almost dark. I'll grab a flashlight."

Both majestic trees had been cut and laid side by side on supporting sawhorse platforms. Both had their bases resting on Halvorsen property while their tops stretched into Lundquist land. White tags wired near the base of each tree named the grower. An additional gold tag attached above recorded the grower's name and the judge's decision. Kris and his dad hurried closer. The Lundquist tag read *First place*.

Kris whispered, "It's true, we won."

They leaped and hugged silently so reporters wouldn't converge. Moments later, Kris turned to his dad.

"I know how much it means to you to win, but I can't do this. It may sound crazy, but our family's fine. We'll keep going forward, but the Halvorsens need this win. I want to change our tag to the Halvorsen tree and switch theirs to ours so they win. Can you be okay with that?"

Lars stared. And sighed. After a long moment, he said, "That's hard, but I see your heart. Go ahead, son."

Kris made the change, and both men walked home.

Minutes later, worried about their future and what she should tell Madison about their attractive job offer, Marcie helped her uncle into the wagon behind the garden tractor and drove to the award area. Using flashlights, they found their name and the winner's tag on their tree. They hugged and beamed and raised hands to heaven for a full minute until Marcie spotted something. At the base of that magnificent winning Balsam fir, two carved hearts intersected with the initials inside that Kris had inscribed years ago, the summer they shared a teenage crush. The only problem was that it was on the Lundquist tree, not the one now labeled Halvorsen. She could barely speak past the giant lump in her throat.

"Uncle Halvor, I don't know how this happened, but there's been a dreadful mistake. This is the Lundquists' tree."

Her uncle's eyebrows shot high. "That can't be. What do you mean?"

"They are the true winners." She helped Halvor come close enough to see for himself.

"Remember that summer in high school when Kris and I had feelings for each other, but you didn't want us together?"

"Yes." He pinched his lips.

"He carved our initials in these joined hearts near the base of their best tree, one of the tall sentinels at the base of their drive." She brushed her hand over the bark. "See? All these years later, the hearts and initials are still there. Someone tagged the wrong tree."

He shook his head. "It's awful, but that's proof, all right. What do you suggest?"

"I'm so sorry. I know your heart was set on winning, but there's only one thing to do. Switch tags before anyone sees."

Halvor gave a slow, sad smile. "You're right, Marcie girl. It's not a true win if the tree isn't ours." He paused. "Could we take a picture of it first, though, to keep for ourselves?"

"Sure, Uncle Halvor." Marcie threw her arms around him before taking a photo and changing the tags.

At 8:30 a.m., people began gathering. Kris rushed to see Marcie before the area filled with spectators.

"Marcie? Wait! I'm sorry, I haven't seen you in forever. I tried the other day, but—"

"I know, photographers everywhere."

"It's important for you to know how much you matter to me. I'm staying in Balsam, and hope you will, too."

"You are? For sure?"

He nodded.

She dropped her hands to her sides. "You have my full attention. What are you saying?"

He felt heat climb his neck. He fumbled in his pocket and pulled out the Christmas ornament ring. "This is ridiculous, but it's all I have. Promise you'll give me time later to do this right."

"Do what, Kris?"

"To say—"

Reporters and photographers surged around them, separating them from each other.

"Are you ready for the awards?" one called.

"Who are you betting on, Lundquist?"

His eyes didn't leave Marcie's. "The best grower will win, and that's the way it should be. We're behind them all the way."

"Are you saying it won't be you?" A bulb flashed.

"It should be," Marcie said. "The Lundquists deserve it."

"Please take your seats, everyone," the chairman called.

"Remember to save me time later," Kris said as he and Marcie moved apart.

By 9 a.m., there was greater commotion and fanfare in the tree award area. All wooden benches were filled, and it was standing room only all the way into the rows of surrounding Christmas trees. Cameras whirred, and flashbulbs popped. Journalists asked questions and talked all at once, sounding like the United Nations in session. The head of the National Christmas Tree Association had flown in to emcee the awards.

The Lundquist and Halvorsen families sat front and center along with townspeople and a crowd of Wisconsinites and

Midwesterners. They were not near enough to read the actual labels on the trees.

"Thanks for getting us recognized," Dave Scholz hollered.

"And bringing in more business," the hardware store owner called.

The NCTA chairman climbed the podium. "Ladies and Gentlemen, what an important day in our history. Drum roll! Without further suspense, we're pleased to announce that this year's supplier of the beautiful tree going to the White House to be decorated by America's First Lady will be a Wisconsin grower. Both top contestants are from Balsam."

"Hear! Hear!" An onlooker shouted as more flashbulbs flashed.

"Round of applause, everyone. I'm pleased to announce this year's winner is Lundquist Christmas Tree Farms! Kris Lundquist? Will you please stand and step forward to receive this award."

Kris jumped to his feet with confusion on his face. "Are you sure? I mean, it's not our tree. When I checked the tags last night, the Halvorsens had won."

The chairman peered down at him. "No mistake, Kris. I'm looking at the winning tree. Your label and gold award tag are right here in front of me."

Kris looked also and saw their winning tags on the same tree where he'd carved the hearts long ago. Where he'd like to carve them all over again right now, deeper. He stood and made his way to the front.

Photographers crowded around him, taking pictures as he approached the chairman. He caught Marcie's eye and mouthed, "I'm sorry."

She flashed a thumb's up. "Fine," she mouthed back. Next to her, Halvor's lips curved in a slight smile.

"How will your tree be going to Washington?" one reporter asked. "will your family go with it?"

"We have to figure that out," Kris said. "We need time to decide ."

A television cameraman shouted, "Will you return to work in New York?"

Kris gazed straight into the camera. "No. I've found everything I want right here in Balsam. Next question?"

Half an hour later, as the furor calmed, Kris reached Marcie. "We weren't supposed to win. I wanted you to."

"We know the wonderful thing you did, Kris. Uncle Halvor and I checked the trees late last night and found our name on yours. It was wrong, so we fixed it."

He rocked on his heels. "Why? I wanted you to win. I mean, how did you know which was which?" Her beautiful eyes pulled him in, and he took a step nearer. If he got any closer, he would drown and his heart would quit beating, but he didn't care.

She closed the distance, too. "I saw the intertwined hearts you carved."

He gripped her hands. "I'd carve them bigger now."

She laughed. "Not if this tree is going to Washington D. C. Then the tree would be about us, not the nation."

"What's wrong with that?" He lifted her hand to his lips.

"So you're not going back to New York."

"Nope. Not when Balsam is so much better. I wanted you to win so you wouldn't go to Madison. You won't, will you?"

"You don't want me to?"

"Absolutely not. I want you right here. With me. Forever. More than any Christmas tree fame or money, I want you." He pulled her into his arms. "I still only have this ring from the top of a Christmas ornament. I put it on my little finger so I wouldn't lose it."

"You're original, at least."

"No other girl anywhere will have one like it. I should have done this long ago. Marcie, I know what I want in life, and it's you. I know where I want to be, right here in Balsam. I love you and want to build my life with you. Wait!" He dropped to one knee. "This feels right. Marcie, will you please marry me and make me the happiest man on this planet?"

She pulled him to his feet. "Absolutely yes." She tilted her face up to his. Their lips met in a sweet, deepening kiss that left them both breathless. A few scattered people applauded, so Kris and Marcie kissed again.

"How soon can marry?" he asked.

"At least not until after Christmas."

"But can we include Christmas fun?"

"I think we should."

"What about Christmas in July? Can we manage that?"

"Kris, that's a great plan. We can have a great start and make it fun for the whole town."

"We'll let your aunt and my mom give us ideas, too."

"They have a million. We can't leave your dad and my uncle out either."

"We won't. We'll make it the happiest July wedding Balsam has ever had!"

"With the best happily-ever-after following it." They sealed their agreement with kiss after kiss.

31

———

With his cane perched next to him, but no walker in sight, Halvor Halvorsen drove his garden tractor down his driveway, across the road, and all the way to the Lundquists' home. He parked near their porch, clambered off, and carefully climbed the steps. After hesitating a moment, he knocked on their door.

Lars opened it. "Halvor! What a nice surprise! Come in."

Halvor leaned on his cane. "No. This is fine." He gestured with his good hand. "May we sit on your porch swing?"

"Sure thing.

"I want to talk to you man to man." Halvor eased himself down.

The swing swayed as Lars sat beside him. "You're making good progress."

"I'm grateful. Hard work, but they say I'll improve more."

"Impressive. And you're getting back into action."

"Yes, but life has benefits in the slow lane. I wanted to save my family and farm, but it seems only the Lord can do that."

"That's wisdom not everybody learns. I don't mind slowing down more myself."

"We can with our kids home." Halvor relaxed and unbuttoned his jacket.

Lars nodded. "They're both prizes."

Halvor shifted his cane to his other hand. "Kris is doing wonders for our farms and Balsam, too. Has he cut ties with New York?"

"He's done some phone work for them, but that's over. He wants to make our businesses grow here."

"That sounds great." Halvor sat up straighter and looked Lars in the eye. "Despite my fussing years back, I'm glad your son and my niece are getting married."

"Lars eyebrows raised. "Even though he's Swedish and she's Norwegian?"

"That can't be helped." Halvor spread open hands. "The Lord decides who's born where."

"Yup, like China. Or Australia."

"I'm glad to be born here. Besides, a good man taught me we're all Scandinavians. We should get along and pull together."

Lars leaned forward. "I like that."

"Yup. Ingrid says I'm coming to my senses." Halvor risked a grin. "Kris is rubbing off on me."

"In good ways?" Lars leaned back against the swing, making it rock.

"Yup. He's a fine man. You and Karin raised him right."

"Thanks." Lars sat up straighter. "We tried."

"Have you heard their wedding plans? They have great ideas."

Lars chuckled. "They do, don't they?"

"Christmas in July? Based on our life here. But I'd like to see those ideas go further."

"What do you mean?"

"What if Balsam had Christmas in July every summer? Pulled out the stops. Make events so fun that people come from all over?"

Lars's eyes widened. "Keep talking."

"But first, something else needs to happen." Halvor pulled a scrolled paper from his pocket. "This is my farm acreage deed after we had to sell half. Yours looks similar. It was all one farm in the beginning. What if you and I signed off on our separate farms and put the land together again in the kids' hands—the way it was meant to be? Except you and I'd stay involved, of course."

"Are you serious? Your face is glowing."

"My heart is, too."

"You've discussed this with Ingrid?"

"She's in favor."

"Do the kids know?"

"Nope. But if you and Karin agree, we could make it a wedding gift. Draw up a new deed. Instead of Halvorsen or Lundquist Farms, call it H & L Christmas Tree Farms. What do you think? Just because *H* comes before *L* in the alphabet, of course."

"It does, doesn't it?"

Both men let the swing's motion rock them forward and back a few times.

"Karin will be for it. That name has a good ring. We don't care whose name comes first."

"I didn't think you would." The men matched smiles.

"Here's what I'm thinking," Halvor said. "No boundary line. Work together and increase efficiency with Kris and Marcie in charge. He's good at business and sales."

Lars leaned closer. "I know. He'll apply big-city ideas to small-town situations, so we all benefit."

"That's right. Marcie can develop her tree seedling nursery and ship quality trees anywhere."

"And keep prices down by doing it here. I agree. Kris will manage well. My skill is maintenance, not numbers."

"We need both. I'm a decent carpenter. I let things go but can swing a hammer again soon."

"Good." Lars smiled. "While planning the wedding

reception, have you heard some of the ideas our wives came up with?"

"A few. Mostly recipes and decorations. I didn't pay much attention."

"They'll hold it in our barn with clog dancing and Swedish and Norwegian food—"

"Nope. Scandinavian," Halvor corrected.

"Yes. But the reception will be so much fun, they talked about keeping some activities going again each summer. Adding a farm-to-market gift shop at least from Balsam Days through Christmas. Maybe year-round."

"That might be good."

They quit rocking.

Lars pulled a small notebook and pen out of his pocket and started writing. "Yeah, Ingrid said besides Christmas trees, wreaths, swags, and decorations, they could offer food items and local products."

"Why not? Like Dave's cheeses, Lisa's cookies, and crafts."

"Yes," Halvor said. "Remember the portable ice cream shoppe here during Balsam days? They were so busy, they sold out of ice cream twice. Kris and Marcie connected with the owner, and he'll set one up at their wedding."

"I like that."

"Me, too. I bet we can think up lots more together, especially with our wives. I'd rather have Karin and Ingrid working here with us than in town."

"For sure. Besides, you and I are getting older." Lars tapped his neighbor's shoulder.

Halvor jerked. "Speak for yourself. I'm not claiming old age for a while yet."

"Agreed, but our reunited farm will prosper. The best days for H & L Christmas Tree Farms are ahead."

"Definitely. We'll need new signs at the road."

"They'll look the same on both sides. Ingrid and Kris can

paint them. Before long, we'll have cute little Christmas tree farmer grandchildren running around."

"Let's not be in too much hurry, but I can't wait." Halvor grinned. "We should start a grandfathers' club and talk things over so we don't buy the same gifts at Christmas."

"Right." Lars's eyes twinkled. "We'll take them fishing. I make good lures."

"So I heard." Halvor flexed his good hand. "I always wanted to try that. Will you show me?"

"Any time. I have plenty of supplies."

"With Kris and Marcie in charge, we can take days off here and there to go fishing, don't you think?"

"Yes. But fill in when they need time off."

"Right."

The men sat in companionable peace as the swing moved a few more times.

"When shall we tell the kids what you have in mind?"

"I'd like to surprise them at the wedding. Put a fancy brand-new title deed in a gift-wrapped box. I'll bet Lisa at the bank could make that happen."

"She can do most things."

Halvor sighed contentment from the depths of his toes. "You know, I'm beginning to remember the reason for the season again. It will start feeling like Christmas every day!"

Lars lifted his shoulders and breathed in deeply. "I can handle that. Say, have you heard of watercross? Some fool put his snowmobile on a lake, gunned it, and made it across. What do you think of that?"

"He did? You say he made it?"

"Not every time, but most times."

"And didn't ruin his machine?"

"Nope."

"He's crazy. But it sounds like fun."

"That's what I think. We should try it."

"On Balsam Lake, but not tell the kids."

"Or our wives. We'll shadow each other with a rescue boat."

"But hope we don't need it."

Both men shook with laughter before Halvor stilled to face Lars.

"I'm sorry about all that anger I had before. I don't even know where it came from."

"Hard times, I'd say, but it doesn't matter. It's ancient history now. Over and done with. Don't even remember it."

Halvor shuddered. "I won't. But you're sure?" His voice cracked. "You forgive me?"

"I did a long time ago when you first got sick. I'm just glad you're recovering now!"

Halvor released a deeper sigh and stood to leave. "That's good to hear."

Lars stood, too. Suddenly, both men embraced, slapping each other's backs and chuckling while tears filled their eyes.

"Look at us old geezers," Lars said.

"We're a pair, but we'll do fine." Halvor grinned and grabbed his hanky. "Christmas tree pollen's flying again. Gets me every time."

"Me, too." Lars swiped his eyes.

"We have good times ahead, neighbor."

"We do indeed. I believe good times are already here."

RECIPES

Lefse, like Norwegian flatbread, developed as an effective way to store wheat or potatoes which otherwise might spoil over harsh winter months. The potato mixture is often made ahead and refrigerated for up to two days before cooking. It is best served fresh and warm but can be wrapped between layers of plastic wrap and refrigerated for a few days. It is made without preservatives so keeps well in the refrigerator for up to a week in airtight containers to prevent it from drying out. If not eaten sooner, store it in the freezer for longer periods. It has become a beloved staple served with a variety of toppings.

Halvor Halvorsen's Norwegian Potato Lefse

1 pound potatoes (or 2 cups mashed potatoes)
1/4 cup unsalted butter at room temperature
1/4 cup heavy cream
1/2 tsp. salt or more to taste
1 to 1 1/2 cups all-purpose flour.

Cover potatoes in water and cook until tender. Mash or press hot potatoes through a potato ricer. Place in a large bowl.

Stir butter, cream, salt, and sugar into the potatoes. Cool to room temperature.

Add flour to the potato mixture.

Pull off small dough pieces to form walnut-size balls.

On a lightly floured counter, bread board, or pastry cloth roll out lefse balls to 1/8" thick.

Cook on a hot griddle (400 degree F or 200 C) until bubbles form and both sides are browned. Cool and serve.

Popular toppings:

- Butter, sugar. and cinnamon
- Jams or jellies
- Powdered sugar and lemon juice
- Buttercream frostings—any flavor
- Caramelized sugar and milk to the desired spreading consistency
- Cream cheese and smoked salmon or shaved ham or similar combinations for savory flavors.
- Cheeses shredded or sliced thin.
- Sour cream, leek, and red onion

Lars Lundquist's Swedish Cardamom Ring

1 package active dry yeast or one level tbsp. fresh cake yeast

1/4 cup warm water (approx. 110 degrees F.)

2 1/2 cups milk (approx.110 degrees F.)

3/4 cup melted butter (then cooled to room temp.)

1 egg

1/2 tsp. salt

1 cup sugar

1 1/2 tsps. cardamom (picked from pods and freshly
ground for the best flavor)
7 cups all-purpose flour

Dissolve the yeast in warm water in a large bowl. Add 1 tsp.
of sugar to be sure the yeast is working.

Stir in warm milk, melted butter, egg, salt, sugar, and
cardamom

Gradually add the flour to form a stiff dough

Turn onto a floured board and knead until smooth (around
ten minutes). Add more flour as needed to prevent sticking.

Place dough in a greased bowl, turning it once to coat all
sides.

Cover and let rise in a warm place until double in size, about
1 1/2 hours.

Punch down dough and divide into six equal parts. Roll out
each part into 24" lengths. Place three lengths side-by-side on a
greased baking sheet and pinch together at one end to make a loose
braid. Then curve to form a ring, pinching the ends together well.

Repeat for the second ring.

Cover and let rise in warm place until almost doubled, about
40 minutes.

Bake in a 350 degree F. oven 35 to 45 minutes until medium
brown. Cool on wire racks.

After cooling for ten minutes, drizzle the ring with icing
Decorate with candied cherries if desired. Lars recommends
adding the cherries.

(Recipe thanks to Jean Ann Carlson Sharpe)

Icing

2 cups powdered sugar
1/4 cup milk
1 tsp. lemon or almond extract

Stir together until smooth

ABOUT THE AUTHOR

In third grade, Delores began composing rhyming stories. Her classmates' approval encouraged her writing. Two of her four award-winning children's books are rhymed adventures.

Delores grew up near Fort Vancouver, Washington, loving its history. Before it was enclosed for safety, she crawled to the original well's edge, appreciating its stone-lined walls built by early hands. To *absorb* history, she's eaten knobby green apples from the Pacific Northwest's oldest apple tree planted by Dr. John McLoughlin. Although he is highly known and revered, Delores found Marguerite's lesser-known life to be a gold mine whose inspiring story needs to be known. Together she and John are known as the Mother and Father of the Pacific Northwest and Marguerite as "the kindest woman in Oregon."

Delores married a Canadian so enjoys U.S. and Canadian citizenships. That also brought her to location sites across

Canada important to this book. Her earlier novel, *Books Afloat,* fictionalizes the true story of a Japanese submarine entering the Columbia River in 1942 with a young woman and crew on a floating library houseboat who fight to stop it.

The Christmas Tree Wars, releasing October 5th, 2021, is a fun Romeo and Juliet style story of two feuding Wisconsin Christmas tree farmers who have lost sight of *the reason for the season.*

Delores loves her doctor sons, families, and five grandchildren and is something she didn't think she'd be—a snowbird dividing her year between Minnesota and Mississippi.

Besides writing, she teaches university classes and enjoys travel, photography, and various hobbies. She also loves connecting with readers and speaking to writing groups and book clubs. Find her blogs, books, and more at delorestopliff.com. Connect on Facebook at Delores Topliff Books.

ALSO BY DELORES TOPLIFF

Books Afloat

Columbia River Undercurrents

Book One

Blaming herself for her childhood role in the Oklahoma farm truck accident that cost her grandfather's life, Anne Mettles is determined to make her life count. She wants to do it all–captain her library boat and resist Japanese attacks to keep America safe. But failing her pilot's exam requires her to bring others onboard.

Will she go it alone? Or will she team with the unlikely but (mostly) lovable characters? One is a saboteur, one an unlikely hero, and one, she discovers, is the man of her dreams.

* * *

Wilderness Wife

by Delores Topliff

Coming in 2022

Can a centuries old love story that changed North American history
encourage others today that true love is still worth fighting for?

WANT MORE CHRISTMAS STORIES?

Candy Cane Wishes and Saltwater Dreams

A collection of Christmas beach romances

by five multi-published authors.

***Mistletoe Make-believe* by Amy Anguish** – Charlie Hill's family thinks his daughter Hailey needs a mom—to the point they won't get off his back until he finds her one. Desperate to be free from their nagging, he asks a stranger to pretend she's his girlfriend during the holidays. When romance author Samantha Arwine takes a working vacation to St. Simon's Island over Christmas, she never dreamed she'd be involved in a real-life romance. Are the sparks between her and Charlie real? Or is her imagination over-acting ... again?

***A Hatteras Surprise* by Hope Toler Dougherty** –Ginny Stowe spent years tending a childhood hurt that dictated her college study and work. Can time with an island visitor with ties to her past heal lingering wounds and lead her toward a happy Christmas ... and more? Ben Daniels intends to hire a new branch manager for a Hatteras Island bank, then hurry back to his promotion and Christmas in Charlotte. Spending time with a beautiful local, however, might force him to adjust his sails.

A Pennie for Your Thoughts **by Linda Fulkerson** –When the Lakeshore Homeowner's Association threatens to condemn the cabin Pennie Vaughn inherited from her foster mother, her only hope of funding the needed repairs lies in winning a travel blog contest. Trouble is, Pennie never goes anywhere. Should she use the all-expenses paid Hawaiian vacation offered to her by her ex-fiancé? The trip that would have been their honeymoon?

Mr. Sandman **by Regina Rudd Merrick** – Events manager Taylor Fordham's happily-ever-after was snatched from her, and she's saying no to romance and Christmas. When she meets two new friends—the cute new chef at Pilot Oaks and a contributor on a sci-fi fan fiction website who enjoys debate—her resolve begins to waver. Just when she thinks she can loosen her grip on thoughts of love, a crisis pulls her back. There's no way she's going to risk her heart again.

Coastal Christmas **by Shannon Taylor Vannatter** – Lark Pendleton is banking on a high-society wedding to make her grandparent's inn at Surfside Beach, Texas the venue to attract buyers. Tasked with sprucing up the inn, she hires Jace Wilder, whose heart she once broke. When the bride and groom turn out to be Lark's high school nemesis and ex-boyfriend, she and Jace embark on a pretend romance to save the wedding. But when real feelings emerge, can they overcome past hurts?